jill marshall moved from the United Kingdom to New Zealand, along with her small daughter and her even smaller mad dog. Her childhood ambition was to become an author, so in 2001 Jill gave up her career at a huge international company to concentrate on writing for children. When not working, writing and being a mum, Jill plays guitar, takes singing lessons and is learning to play the drum kit she has set up in the garage. One day she might even sing in a band again . . .

D0201578

Also by Jill Marshall

jane blonde, sensational spylet★
jane blonde spies trouble
jane blonde, twice the spylet
jane blonde, the perfect spylet
(for world book day)
jane blonde, spylet on ice

Look out for more
jane blonde
adventures

★*also available in audio*

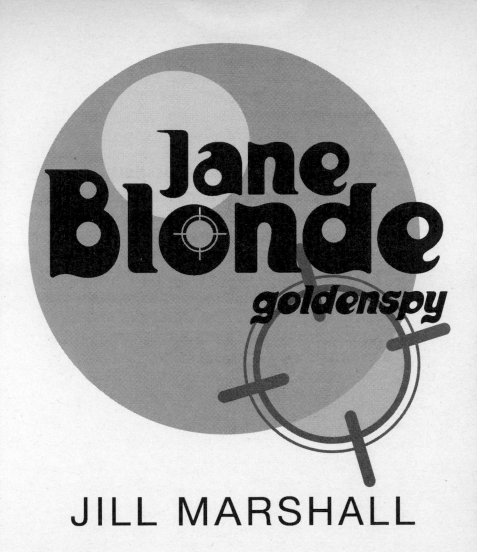

Jane Blonde
goldenspy

JILL MARSHALL

MACMILLAN CHILDREN'S BOOKS

First published 2007 by Macmillan Children's Books
a division of Macmillan Publishers Limited
20 New Wharf Road, London N1 9RR
Basingstoke and Oxford
www.panmacmillan.com

Associated companies throughout the world

ISBN 978-0-230-53244-1

Copyright © Jill Marshall 2008

The right of Jill Marshall to be identified as the
author of this work has been asserted by her in accordance
with the Copyright, Designs and Patents Act 1988.

All rights reserved. No part of this publication may be
reproduced, stored in or introduced into a retrieval system, or
transmitted in any form, or by any means (electronic, mechanical,
photocopying, recording or otherwise), without the prior written
permission of the publisher. Any person who does any unauthorized
act in relation to this publication may be liable to criminal
prosecution and civil claims for damages.

1 3 5 7 9 8 6 4 2

A CIP catalogue record for this book is available from
the British Library.

Typeset by Nigel Hazle
Printed and bound in Great Britain by Mackays of Chatham plc, Kent

This book is sold subject to the condition that it shall not,
by way of trade or otherwise, be lent, resold, hired out,
or otherwise circulated without the publisher's prior consent
in any form of binding or cover other than that in which
it is published and without a similar condition including this
condition being imposed on the subsequent purchaser.

so many thank-yous, as ever. to rachel, talya, dom and the technical team at macmillan. for the first time we hit a few snags with our global writing and editing, but we got through! angie and chris, so glad you're here — we'll miss you, chris! to glenys, g-mamma high-fives and hugs for your constant support and superb advisory emails. and especially for all those spylets who keep asking when the next jb's coming . . . tpy eixj.

for ace spylet anna m.

contents

It had taken all his strength, every ounce of his extraordinary intelligence, to extract himself from the Earth. Now he had to be free of it – forever. Free from the cloying cold that numbed his thoughts and his movements. Free from the pitiful, powerless race who dared, somehow, to condemn him. And free, by whatever means it took, from the SPIs who tried at every turn to stop him, irritating him like mosquitoes, thwarting even his most brilliant manoeuvres.

As for Jane Blonde . . . the mere thought of her made his internal organs cramp with bitter rage. She was the most aggravating of all. Even more so than her conceited, know-it-all father.

But she wouldn't stop him this time. All the Jane Blondes in the world would not be enough to spoil this plan. He had full control, right at his fingertips – or the tips of his tentacles, since Blonde had turned him into this mutant monster.

No matter. He laughed quietly, the full beam of

jane blonde, goldenspy

his gaze taking in the scene before him, the scene he would soon destroy. It was only a matter of time now. Just a matter of time . . .

1 zoo's news

The last week of the school year had come around amazingly quickly. And it wasn't just the speed at which time had passed that had been amazing, thought Janey Brown as she waited in the queue for the coach, pulling her hat down further to stop the sun burning her nose. The year had quite simply been out of this world.

'Don't sit at the back,' said her best friend, Alfie, giving her a shove. 'Those goons will just want to wave at people out of the back window. And not there either,' he added, shuddering as he saw which seat Janey had been about to slide into. 'Too near Mum.'

'Your mum's coming?' Janey was surprised. Alfie's mum was the headmistress of Winton School, but as she didn't have a class of her own she didn't normally go on school trips with the pupils.

'Are you kidding?' Alfie plonked himself next to Janey. 'Her two favourite pupils are going –

that's you and me, in case you hadn't realized – on our last ever school trip from Winton. And where are we going?'

'Solfari Lands,' said Janey with a grin.

No wonder Mrs Halliday couldn't resist. Solfari Lands was the wildlife park operated by Janey's own father, Boz Brilliance Brown, super-SPI, master of disguise and head of his own spying organization, Solomon's Polifications Investigations – or SPI. His team included Mrs Halliday and Alfie, otherwise known as Agent Halo and Spylet Al Halo; Janey's exuberant SPI: Kid Educator – or SPI:KE – who went by the name of G-Mamma, and various other spies and Spylets, with Jane Blonde, Sensational Spylet, proving to be the greatest of them all.

Janey still found it hard to believe that when she stepped into the Wower, the super-charged spy shower in G-Mamma's Spylab, as an ordinary, mousie-haired schoolgirl, she emerged as her platinum-blonde, multi-gadgeted alter ego, Jane Blonde. But it was true. And that was what had made the year so completely incredible – along with the various gadgets she'd employed, the friendships she'd established and the death-defying missions she'd been hurled on to protect her father, her fellow SPIs and Spylets, and even the Earth itself, from destruction at the hands of the mad scientific genius – and rogue spy – Copernicus. Who also happened to be Alfie's father.

Mrs Halliday clambered up the coach steps and clapped her hands. 'Well, boys and girls, here we are . . . Your very last trip before you all go your separate ways after the summer holidays. Let's make the most of it. And, Jake Bell,' she said loudly to one of the 'goons' on the back seat, 'if you even think of sticking your tongue out at people, I'll make you stay with me at Winton for another year.'

Nothing gets past Agent Halo! thought Janey.

She smiled at her head teacher as she walked by, counting heads. Mrs Halliday's hand paused over Janey's hair, then she dropped her hand in a sudden, furtive flick and moved on down the bus. Janey looked down to find a note in her lap.

She opened it eagerly and read it to Alfie in a whisper. 'Lunch for you and A with your father. 12.30. Usual place. I'll cover.' Mrs Halliday had signed off with a flat oval shape – a halo.

Janey was so excited she nearly jumped out of her seat. Instead she settled for grabbing her friend by the elbow. 'Alfie! My dad's here!'

'So it seems,' said Alfie. 'Wonder who he'll be this time?'

'Hmm. Good question.' Over the course of the missions that Janey had completed, her father had turned up either as himself (dark-haired, blue-eyed Boz Brown) or as the version of himself he'd created by going through the dangerous Crystal

5

Clarification Process – tall, sandy-haired, brown-eyed Abe Rownigan. And he had yet another alter ego: Solomon Brown, his own completely invented brother. Janey gave herself a little squeeze. She didn't care which body he turned up in. It was enough that he was going to be there.

The sun beat down on the coach windows as they meandered their way further into the surrounding countryside. The usual place, thought Janey, fanning herself absently with the note from Mrs Halliday. She must mean the Spylab hidden away beneath the Amphibian House, under the holographic North American wood frogs that had inspired her father's first experiments. Only true SPI members would know its location, and Janey could hardly stop herself from running straight there as the coach pulled up in the car park.

'Steady,' said Alfie, seeing how excited she was. 'It's only eleven o'clock.'

'I know,' moaned Janey. 'It's so frustrating. Imagine having your dad so close and not being able to see him . . . oh. Sorry.'

Alfie shrugged at the mention of his father. Last time he'd seen him, Copernicus had been Satispied, SPInamited and Wowed by Jane Blonde, pretty much all at the same time – and the results had not been pretty. Alfie's evil father was now a revolting squid-like creature, whom the SPI team had sent to his death in the depths of the earth. 'Not seeing my father is a very good thing, believe me.'

'Oh, look,' said Janey, changing the subject. 'Monkeys! Aren't they cute?'

The class stood back and watched as several cages were unloaded from the back of a gigantic truck. There were tiny marmosets and lemurs, furry black chimpanzees and two vast crates, each containing a bored-looking, marmalade-coloured orang-utan. 'Don't touch,' warned one of the men as the class gathered around. 'Some of these can give you a nasty bite.'

Janey looked at the nearest chimp. He was cuddled up against a slightly bigger chimpanzee and didn't look capable of hurting a fly, let alone a person. Her heart went out to him and, unthinkingly, she gave him a tiny wave. 'Hello, little chimp.'

The chimp looked back at her with shiny round eyes and suddenly moved his hand in a circle. Janey gasped. 'He waved at me!' She grabbed Alfie's arm and pointed at the cage. 'That one! I waved at him and he did a . . . a circle thing back at me.'

'A circle thing?' Alfie looked closely at the two chimpanzees. 'I think he was just lifting his . . . what is it, a hand or paw? Anyway, look, he was just picking out the other one's fleas. That's disgusting,' he said loudly to the chimp, who blinked at him solemnly and then carried on combing through his neighbour's coat.

7

'You're probably right,' said Janey, a little disappointed. 'Oh well. Let's go and look at the rhinos.'

They wandered around the wildlife park, ambling in the sunshine in a great loop that took them past hippos, rhinos and tigers, past enclosures of deer, impala and zebra, then down a hill into the tropical-bird aviary. The next stop was the Amphibian House. Janey checked her watch. 12.20. Not long now before she could see her dad.

Sure enough, Mrs Halliday shot her a quick, knowing glance before calling all the children to her. 'It's about time we had some lunch. The picnic area's just behind those trees.' She stood like a traffic warden, arms out, waving the class through the gap in the trees until Janey and Alfie were the only ones left. 'Back here in forty-five minutes,' she muttered out of the side of her mouth, before marching across the grass towards the picnic area.

As Janey pushed through the doors of the Amphibian House her heart began to thud with anticipation. Last time she had been here she'd been trapped in the Spylab by the evil Sinerlesse leader, Ariel. Janey was now ten times the Spylet she had been on her first mission. She pressed the red eye of a model tree frog and stepped on to the cushion of air at the top of the entry tube that led down into her father's Spylab.

Janey and Alfie scrambled to their knees in the stark light of the lab and looked around for her father.

'There you are,' said a deep voice, and suddenly Janey was wrapped in a warm hug, her nose pressed into a salmon-pink Solfari Lands polo shirt.

Her father held her at arm's length, and Janey looked up at the crinkly brown eyes and flashing grin of Abe Rownigan. 'You look well,' he said gently.

'So do you,' said Janey, her smile so wide that her eyes had become slits and she could hardly see.

Abe reached over and shook Alfie's hand. 'Al, good to see you.'

'You too. Thanks for inviting me for lunch,' said Alfie. 'Sir,' he added as an afterthought, going slightly pink.

'Ah, yes. Lunch.' Abe looked around the laboratory, rubbing his hands through his hair so it stood up in curls. 'I forgot about that. I could check the fridge. G-Mamma might have filled it up last time she was here.'

'It doesn't matter. We've got our sandwiches with us.' Janey jostled her backpack around so he could see, and Abe smiled.

'Great. Sandwiches it is. You eat,' he said, leading them to one of the workbenches, 'and I'll talk.'

Janey knew that her father put himself in danger whenever he came out of hiding. He must have something very important to share with her and Alfie.

Abe was pacing around the bench, and the atmosphere was electric. What was on his mind?

'Sandwich?' Janey offered.

'Did your mum make them?' Abe grinned. Jean Brown's lack of kitchen skills was legendary in their family. Of course, she had other legendary skills, namely the ones she'd used as super-SPI, Gina Bellarina, before she'd been brain-wiped into a dull but worthy existence as Jean Brown: cleaner, businesswoman and mum.

'I made them,' Janey said with a smile.

Abe shook his head anyway. 'I'm too fired up to eat, to be honest.'

'Has something happened, sir?' Alfie opened his lunchbox and rusltled a packet of crisps anxiously. 'You don't think that my da—'

'No,' said Abe, looking directly at Alfie. 'There's no evidence that Copernicus has resurfaced. But I'm going to need your help guarding this Spylab.'

Janey and Alfie both sat forward eagerly. Something *was* afoot, and that meant one thing – a new mission.

Abe paused, staring at his feet as though the enormity of this mission weighed him down. 'I've discovered something – something enormous. A . . . process, I suppose you'd call it.'

'Like Crystal Clarification?' said Janey breathlessly. Her blood was racing through her veins, nervous excitement mounting with every word.

Her father nodded. 'Yes. But bigger. Bigger than Crystal Clarification *and* the Nine Lives theory *and* the cloning process.' He ticked off his scientific discoveries on his fingers. 'This is . . . extreme. It could affect the whole of mankind.'

Janey held her breath, eyes shining. Alfie gasped, a crisp halfway to his wide-open mouth.

Abe leaned in close. 'This has to remain top secret. It's a Revolution.'

Janey's gaze faltered for a moment. The only revolutions she'd ever heard of involved guns and battles. 'You're starting a war?'

'No, no,' said her father quickly. 'That's the name of the new process I've discovered.'

'Revolution,' whispered Janey.

She exchanged glances with Alfie. Even before they'd heard more, they both knew the truth.

This mission was going to be their biggest yet.

barmy army

The second Janey got home, she muttered an excuse to her mum and charged up the stairs to her bedroom. She closed the door behind her and made straight for the fireplace. As soon as she pressed the wall at the ten-past-two position, the panel at the back of the hearth slid upwards and Janey dropped to her hands and knees and crawled, army style, through the opening. Going through this secret passage to G-Mamma's Spylab next door was now second nature.

She found G-Mamma hard at work, painting a portrait of Trouble. He'd clearly been through the Wower. His eyes gleamed like bright emeralds, go-faster stripes glistened along the sides of his body and his tail bristled thick and glossy like a great golden feather. G-Mamma had also draped a yellow feather boa around his neck and garbed him in a neat leather waistcoat. They both glanced up as Janey entered the Spylab, Trouble looking rather pleased with himself, and G-Mamma daubed in a rainbow of paint. 'Whaddya think, Zany Janey?' she said, spinning the portrait around.

It was surprisingly good in a completely crazy kind of way, and Janey had to stifle a laugh. 'It's . . . er . . . great. But listen: you'll never guess what happened at Solfari Lands.'

'Well, let me try . . . your father turned up and told you about a meeting at midnight tonight with some of the other SPIs and Spylets?' G-Mamma pointed to the pineapple-sized SPI Visualator around her neck. 'Agent Halo filled me in.'

'It's so exciting!' said Janey. 'He's made a new discovery and it's enormous and we're going to have to patrol Solfari Lands and guard his secret lab!'

G-Mamma looked down at her lilac ballgown and huge, specially made glass slippers. 'Your father had better not make us wear that revolting uniform. A polo shirt? In *prawn* pink? Not for me, no sireee!'

Janey rolled her eyes but patted her SPI:KE's arm soothingly. 'Don't worry. We'll be in our spy gear. I'll come back to Wow up later.'

'Right you are, Blondette,' said G-Mamma, checking the clock. 'We'll meet in seven hours. Your dad's improved the Satispy system so we'll zap ourselves over there. Now, go and do your daughterly duties and keep Mumsy out of the way.' She pointed to the screen projected on to the massive fridge: next door, Jean Brown was heading up the stairs.

Janey dived for the fireplace tunnel and just man-aged to get to her own hearth as her mother entered the room with a pile of clothes. 'Put these away, please, and then we'll . . .'

Jean Brown stopped suddenly and ducked her head, staring directly behind Janey into the fireplace. Janey winced. She hadn't had time to close the panel between her room and the Spylab; any minute now her mum would discover what she was up to every night. They'd move house. Her spy life would be over . . .

'What is . . . ?' Her mum glared at her. 'How did you get *paint* in your fireplace?'

Janey spun around. A slick of magenta paint was snaking its way across the hearth, but to her great relief the passageway was closed off. G-Mamma must have activated the panel for her, spilling a pot of paint in the process. Smiling regretfully, she said, 'Sorry, Mum. I . . . there was a spider in there and I threw the nearest thing at it.'

Jean tutted. 'Honestly, Janey. Well, make sure you clear it up.' She dropped the laundry stack on to the end of Janey's bed and sat down next to it. 'Just one more day before the summer holidays, and we haven't orga-nized a thing. Shall we book a holiday?' She beamed at Janey, who wondered once more how she was going to let her mum down without hurting her feelings.

'Oh, I don't know . . . the weather's nice here. We could just hang around at home, couldn't we?' At

home, near Solfari Lands, available for SPI work . . .
They couldn't go away *now*.

Jean looked a little disappointed, then shrugged.
'All right. I've got some time off work. Joy's going to
stand in for me. Why don't we do a few day trips?'

Janey nodded and gave her mum a hug. 'Day trips
sound perfect. The one to the wildlife park today was
fantastic.'

'OK. Think of some places you'd like to go,' said
Jean, getting up from the bed. 'And tea's ready in half
an hour.'

It was really impossible to fathom, thought Janey
over her sausage, chips and baked beans, how Jean
Brown could be so ignorant of Janey's other life,
particularly when she herself had once been a super-
SPI. Rather ashamed, Janey realized how good she
had become at acting, playing a role. Or *lying*, as her
mother might call it.

But any guilt Janey felt about hiding her double
life was soothed away a few hours later as the Wower's
robotic arms massaged her bony shoulders, encased
her in silver Lycra and kitted her out in Fleet-feet, Girl-
gauntlet and slender black Ultra-gogs. She felt a surge
of excitement and power as a mirage of swirling droplets spun her hair into a platinum ponytail, and a cool
female voice informed her, 'Jane Blonde, Sensational
Spylet: you are ready for action.'

G-Mamma was already Wowed, a vision in

15

striped fuchsia and a veiled turban that made her look rather like a fancy marquee. 'That's better,' she said approvingly, looking Janey up and down. 'I'm rather fond of Jane the Blonde.'

Janey sensed a rap coming on, so she quickly scooped up Trouble, entered the coordinates for Solfari Lands and pressed the Satispy remote. The Spycat disintegrated before their eyes and shot up through the skylight in tiny pieces, like bubbles in a bottle of fizzy drink.

'You next,' said G-Mamma, taking the remote.

Janey stationed herself where Trouble had been standing and waited for the peculiar pins-and-needles sensation as her cells split away from each other and then zinged up to a satellite in space. As ever, a wave of nausea hit as she neared the satellite, then she was streaming back down to Earth in a river of cells, which joined together so her body reconnected before her eyes, and the floor of the Solfari Lands Spylab loomed up at her.

They were among the last to arrive. Other SPIs and Spylets were leaning against the workbenches, chatting quietly as G-Mamma plummeted through the skylight, which, by day, just looked like a square of turf next to the Amphibion House.

Janey looked around. Alfie and his mum were there, of course, and several other families of SPIs she'd already met: Titian Ambition, known as Tish, and her mother,

Magenta, in their trademark red SPIsuits; Leaf Erikssen, in racing green, along with his father, Ivan; and Eagle and Peregrine with their Spylet twins, Rook and . . .

Blackbird? Janey did a double take. Blackbird had disappeared on their last mission and was almost certainly responsible for feeding information to Copernicus! Tish was also glaring at the Spylet in the shimmering, feather-covered black SPIsuit. Janey almost grinned in spite of her shock: Tish could never keep her feelings to herself.

'Welcome, everyone,' said Abe, entering through a door at the back of the lab. 'G-Mamma, could you close off the skylight?'

G-Mamma pushed a button under the little window, and the square of earth dropped back into place.

'Thank you. You'll all need to make sure it's the first thing you do when you arrive for patrol.'

'Patrol?' said Leaf, his Scandinavian accent as delicate as his appearance. 'Like in the army?'

'If you like. Let me explain myself more clearly.' Abe pointed to the door he had just come through. 'That room is the location of my most amazing – and frightening – discovery so far. It's a process I'm calling Revolution. I'm sorry that I can't tell you any more about it. I think the less you know, the better it will be if you are captured.'

'And . . . like, tortured?' said Alfie quietly.

Abe sighed. 'I sincerely hope it never

17

comes to that, but there is always the danger that our enemies will try to pressure you into telling them what you know. However, for *my* safety and the protection of the Revolution secret, I want a guard around the Spylab twenty-four/seven. It's not your most exciting mission, I'm afraid. But it could be your most vital.'

Everyone was quiet as they wondered what miraculous discovery Abe had made. Suddenly a peculiar chattering noise cut through the silence. It's coming from behind that door, thought Janey. She looked at her father, her eyebrows raised.

Abe cleared his throat. 'No one is to go through there,' he said with cool emphasis, pausing after every word. 'Now, Halo, can I leave the organization of this mission to you?'

'Of course,' said Mrs Halliday. 'I'll draw up a rota. School timetables, you know – I'm pretty good at that kind of thing.'

For the first time since they had arrived, Abe's face relaxed into a genuine film-star smile. 'Perfect. We'll start tonight, if that's OK. Everyone to take their times from Halo.'

'Me first, Maisie!' yelled G-Mamma, swirling her hips like a deep pink tornado. 'Blonde and I will do the first stint. If you like . . .' she added, as Magenta and Ivan frowned in her direction.

Mrs Halliday nodded. 'That's fine. There are twelve of us, so there will be four spies on each of the

three eight-hour shifts. Blonde, Al Halo, G-Mamma
and I will take this 10 p.m. to 6 a.m. shift, so Blonde
is back home before her mother suspects anything.
Then Leaf and Ivan, Tish and Magenta – are you
OK for 6 a.m. until 2 p.m.? And then the Bird
family, you'll do two till ten. We'll rotate after a
week.'

Janey looked around at the people in the room.
Her father was watching everyone's reactions with
great interest, and he wasn't the only one. Blackbird's
dark gaze flicked anxiously from one person to the
next. Janey had to say something.

She raised her hand slowly. 'Um, I don't want to
be mean, but we all know there's a double agent in the
room.' Nobody said anything, although Blackbird's
head dropped instantly. 'Blackbird, you gave my eSPI-
drills to Copernicus so that he could find out the exact
formation of the centre of the earth. Why should we
trust you?'

To her surprise, Blackbird burst into tears. 'I
didn't know what he wanted them for. I nearly caused
the whole Earth to be destroyed!'

'Why did you do it?' asked Janey gently.

Blackbird sniffed noisily and shook her head, looking more bird-like than ever. 'I was stupid, that's why.
I was just trying to be important, like all the rest of you
are. I wasn't picked for the mission, and I wasn't very
good at anything, and—'

'I was not picked for the mission either,' said Leaf bitterly. 'But did I go become a traitor? No. I, Leaf Erikssen, directly descended from the man who first discovered America, was not chosen, and still I acted with respect. Why could you not do that?'

'You're descended from Columbus?' said Alfie incredulously. 'Wasn't he Spanish or something?'

'No, no, no. From Leif Erikssen, the Viking,' Leaf snapped as he turned back to Blackbird. 'So?'

'C-Copernicus said I could be his chief Spylet if I just got him your eSPIdrills. I'm . . . so sorry.' And she burst into racking sobs. Rook, who up until then had been looking rather disgusted, patted his sister awkwardly on the arm.

Abe held up a hand. 'Look, I knew this would be a concern for you, but I have spoken to Blackbird and I am quite confident that she made an error of judgement. And that she is now completely loyal to our cause.'

'I am! I really, really am,' wailed Blackbird, wiping her nose on her feathery arm.

'So can we all agree to forget about that incident?' Abe looked at each of his spies and Spylets in turn, Leaf first, and they all stared intently at Blackbird and then nodded slowly.

Janey suddenly felt sorry for Blackbird. She'd made a few wrong decisions herself in the past, guided by her emotions rather than by logic. She'd even been tempted to give up spying altogether, simply because she hadn't been chosen for the last mission either. And if her dad trusted the other Spylet . . . She smiled at Blackbird. 'OK,' she said softly. 'All forgotten.'

And so the first patrol settled in for the evening, and the mission – to protect Revolution – began.

Abe disappeared through his mysterious door as Jane and Alfie took up their stations outside. Alfie was still muttering about Leaf. Jane had noticed before that he didn't like it when someone else appeared to know something he didn't. 'Everyone knows Columbus dis-covered America. Leaf's totally wrong . . .'

'Alfie,' said Janey softly, 'I think we've got more important things to worry about than *that*.'

And she was right.

As soon as Janey got into school the next morning she was called to Mrs Halliday's office. Alfie was already there, and he shrugged, mystified, as Janey walked in.

'We're needed back at the Solfari Lands lab,' said Mrs Halliday briefly. 'We'll have to go as soon as school finishes. Thank goodness it's a half-day today.'

'What's happened?' Janey thought instantly of her father. 'Is Dad OK?'

'He's fine, but he's not very happy,' said Mrs Halliday. 'During the handover between our shift and the next, something went missing – something vital to Revolution.'

'Well, we haven't got it,' said Alfie indignantly. 'Whatever *it* is,' he added hastily.

Mrs Halliday looked grim but would say no more. Janey was bursting with questions and worries but had to contain herself for the rest of the morning. What was the mysterious stolen object? Were they under suspicion? Whatever had disappeared *had* gone missing just as their shift was going home. Surely her father wouldn't suspect *them*? Would he?

monkey mayhem

'Someone stole a monkey?' Janey gazed at her father, perplexed. 'How would they steal a monkey? And, um, *why?*' But then Janey remembered the noise they had heard last night . . . the noise that had come from her father's Revolution room. *A monkey . . .*

'When did you notice it was gone?' said Alfie sensibly.

'Eight o'clock this morning,' said Abe.

'Aha!' Alfie jumped to his feet and paced the room, a mini Sherlock Holmes in school uniform. 'So it could have disappeared at any time during the night. It could have been on either shift, or even before we all gathered here at midnight.'

Abe nodded. 'You're right. Which means someone may well know about Revolution . . .' Janey had never seen her father look so grave.

'You know what does seem weird though,' said Janey suddenly. 'The one person we have most reason to be worried about wasn't on either of those shifts. Maybe Blackbird arranged it especially so that all the suspicion would fall on us.'

The others looked at her, one or two of them starting to nod their agreement. 'That is right,' said Leaf. 'She has set us up.'

'It doesn't make sense,' said Abe shortly. 'Blackbird is desperate to be one of us again. She'd know she'd be the first one to fall under the spotlight.'

'And anyway, old Copper Knickers is dead,' said G-Mamma. 'There's nobody to pull her strings.'

That was true. They all looked glumly at each other, unable to come up with any solutions or sensible suggestions. And just as the atmosphere became completely gloomy, Janey voiced the most horrible thought of all. 'Maybe he's not.'

'Maybe he's not *what*, Jane the Insane?' G-Mamma's bright blue eye peered at her through the hole of a doughnut, purchased from the Solfari Lands Cafe as they'd arrived.

Janey swallowed slowly. 'Maybe Copernicus isn't dead. I know he should be, buried deep down in the Antarctic in a broken rocket, but SPUD Nik managed to get out . . .' Her robot penguin had been trapped with Copernicus, but he'd escaped.

'No,' said Alfie, almost spitting out the word. 'Not again. He was meant to be dead after you SPInamited him in the Wower.'

'And he wasn't.' Janey looked around at the solemn faces. 'I bet he's free. Somehow.'

Her father had already turned to the computer as G-Mamma slammed a fist into her other hand. 'Oh, you just lemme at him,' she growled. 'I'll squish that squid, righty almighty. Like this!' She leaped out of her seat and mimed the actions to her rap:

I'll squish him, uh-huh uh-huh,
I'll squish him dead . . .
By sitting, uh-huh uh-huh,
On his squiddy head.'

She looked so ferocious that no one dared laugh. Then Abe looked up from the computer. His face was ashen.

'It's not good news,' he said.

He swivelled the computer screen round to show them the article he'd found on an international news website. 'Mutant Colossal Squid sighted in warm waters,' ran the headline.

Holidaymakers surfing off the Florida coast near Titusville were staggered to find an unusual creature sharing the sea with them. Several eyewitnesses have sworn that they barely avoided being wrapped up in the tentacles of a strange octopus-like creature. Said Michael Palfryman of the University of West

Florida: 'It really sounds like a Colossal Squid, which is pretty amazing – most other sightings have been in the dark, freezing waters of the Antarctic, like the vast specimen picked up by fishermen near New Zealand recently.' The creature is thought to have been damaged in a fight, perhaps with a shark, as one eye is barely visible while the other is huge and yellow. Coastguards are warning swimmers and surfers to be vigilant.

Janey's worst fear had just been realized. Copernicus was back. 'That's got to be him,' she said. 'Usually seen in the Antarctic, one eye bigger than the other . . .'

'But what's he doing in *Florida*?' asked Tish.

Alfie opened a new packet of chewing gum and started chomping furiously. 'Maybe he's having a holiday,' he said hopefully. 'Must be tiring, after all, when you keep . . .' he chewed a bit harder, '. . . escaping . . . DEATH.'

But Janey knew – they all knew – that the truth had to be more sinister. Wherever Copernicus was, there was danger. And wherever danger was, thought Janey, someone else should be.

Jane Blonde.

'I have to go to Florida,' she said decisively.

Abe stared at her for a moment, visibly struggling between his wish to keep his daughter safe and the need to get his best spies on the job to tackle his arch-enemy. He thought out loud: 'He's luring us to him . . . he's recruited someone to steal from me while he's busy preparing to wreak havoc in America. Now it's like he's calling us . . . I can't let you go . . . But we need to know exactly how far he's got with Revolution . . .' Suddenly he nodded. 'Yes. Janey, I need you to go. But not on your own.'

Alfie let out a low growl, which startled everyone. 'I'll go too.' He glared at Leaf, who'd dared to look at him. 'My father, my problem.'

'All right, Alfie,' said his mother. 'But I'm coming as well.'

'And me!' yelped G-Mamma.

The others all looked about to volunteer so Abe tapped on the table to get everyone's attention. 'I do still need some of you here,' he said with a rueful smile. 'G-Mamma, if you and Leaf could take over the night shift, I'd be very grateful. Magenta and Tish, the early shift. And, Ivan, I'm going to need your cell-tracing expertise in this new process, if that's all right with you.'

The SPIs and Spylets agreed readily, although G-Mamma and Leaf still looked a tiny bit mutinous. Both hated to be left out of the most exciting – and dangerous – part of the mission.

'We'll catch whoever's monkey-stealing,' G-Mamma muttered in a loud aside to Leaf, determined to make their work matter every bit as much as the Florida trio's. 'I'll get Agent Dubbo Seven over from Oz – he's good at tracking and what have you. We'll track 'em and sack 'em.'

'Track them and sack them,' agreed Leaf earnestly.

So, with the arrangements in place, they all headed off to their various home locations to prepare for the next part of the mission. As they pulled up near her house Mrs Halliday eyed Janey in the mirror. 'So how do we deal with your mum this time, Janey?'

Janey groaned. Her mum. Six weeks' holiday ahead of them, time off work, day trips planned, and now Janey was going to disappear.

And suddenly she decided. This time it was going to be different.

'Just leave Mum to me,' she said with a smile. 'But send us an email to let me know where we're staying.'

Still grinning, Janey ran into the house. She threw her arms around her mum and gave her a big squeeze.

'You must have had a good last day,' said her mother breathlessly.

'I did,' said Janey, although she wasn't about to reveal why. 'And I've changed my mind. Let's go on holiday.'

'Really?' said Jean, pleased and very excited.

Janey nodded. 'I'd really love to go to Florida. Tonight!'

'Well, we don't need to . . .' Jean Brown stopped, and then threw her hands in the air. 'Oh, why not? I'm sure I can get something on the Internet.'

Strangely enough, the Hallidays had decided to do exactly the same thing and had emailed suggesting two side-by-side villas, next to a pool and close to all the main attractions. They'd even managed to get four seats on a very small plane leaving that very evening. Oh, and Mrs Halliday was happy to book the whole thing on her credit card, and Janey's mum could just pay her back. Sometimes, thought Janey, having a dad who was head of a spying organization definitely had its perks. As her slightly bewildered mum started to pack, Janey ran upstairs to tell G-Mamma.

'OK,' said G-Mamma sniffily. 'But don't you go getting sunstroke, and do not have too much of a good time without me.'

Janey laughed. 'I'm going on a mission, remember, not a *holiday*.'

'Hmph. Well, choppity-chop, we'd better get you ready,' said G-Mamma.

The Wower door hissed closed behind Janey.

'Wow me,' she said firmly. Then she closed her eyes dreamily as the magical transforming mist descended around her.

When she stepped out a few minutes later, G-Mamma squinted at her and then stumbled around the lab screaming, 'My eyes, my cherry-pie eyes – I'm blinded!' She stopped abruptly. 'You look like an Oscar statuette. Blondette, the Oscarette!'

'What are you talking about?' Janey turned to look at herself in the long mirrored door of the Wower . . . and clapped a hand over her mouth. G-Mamma was right! Janey's silver Jane Blonde outfit had been exchanged for a gleaming golden SPIsuit, like the wetsuits she had seen surfers wear. In place of her Ultra-gogs was a pair of large coppery sunglasses, with diamanté trim along the frame. On her feet were summery flip-flops, golden to match her SPIsuit, while her ponytail, sleek and platinum blonde, peeked out of a very cool khaki-coloured cap.

'What happened?' she asked, stunned.

G-Mamma rifled around in a cupboard as she explained: 'Golden SPIsuit. Perfect for the summer! And I guess it was time you had an upgrade! Now, your sunglasses function just like your Ultra-gogs, apart from the diamond glass-cutter studs in the frames. Might be useful – you never know. Groovy cap – that's a PERSPIRE: a Personal SPI Remote Educator, or a tiny computer to you. And, finally, those flip-flops. The new Fleet-feet design – we're calling them Flip-Flop-Fleet-feet. Four-Fs for short. Just as fast, just as springy, but the left one works like a circular saw if you whizz it along on its side. Oh, and the right doubles as a Frisbee. Perfect for the beach.'

Janey couldn't stop staring at her reflection, and then she started to giggle. If her outfit was this over the top, what was Alfie's going to be like?

Suddenly G-Mamma stopped rummaging. 'You'll be needing this. A surfboard-sized Aeronautical SPI Conveyor!'

'Wow,' was just about all that Janey could manage.

Anyway, it was time to go. Pushing the surfboard ASPIC through the fireplace passage, Janey turned and gave G-Mamma a quick hug.

'Send me a postcard,' said her SPI:KE in a small voice, two of her several chins wobbling dangerously. 'And don't worry – I'll take good care of Trouble.'

'Thanks, G-Mamma. I'll contact you on the SPIV. Bye, Twubs! I'll miss you!'

An hour and a half later her mum, Mrs Halliday, Alfie (in blue silky board shorts, rash shirt and Four-Fs) and Janey (with a skirt and T-shirt over the golden glamour of her spy outfit) climbed the steps to the plane. We look exactly like what Mum thinks we are: tourists, on holiday. As if, thought Janey.

4 villa del sol

The holiday villas were in a tiny complex in Orlando – four tall terraces around a sparkling kidney-shaped pool, each painted a different ice-cream shade: vanilla, strawberry, pistachio and coffee. Jean Brown's eyes widened as the chauffeured car pulled through the great iron gates.

'Villa del Sol,' she read aloud as they passed the sign. 'Villa of the sun, I suppose. Nice. Maisie, you really did get an amazing deal with this place.'

Janey knew that 'Sol' had more to do with Solomon Brown, one of her father's identities, but she just smiled sweetly at her mum and waited for the car to stop. It was dark, almost midnight, in Florida despite the fact that they had just flown for ten hours through the night, but the chauffeur seemed more than happy to lug their suitcases and surfboards to their respective holiday homes and flick on the lights for them. 'Thank you,' said Jean, self-consciously holding out a few dollars as a tip.

The chauffeur waved it away. 'No problem. Courtesy of Villa del Sol, ma'am. Now make sure you use that air-conditioning – it's so hot during the day it's a wonder the pool doesn't bubble.'

'Erm, thank you,' said Jean again, and the chauffeur tipped his hat at Janey and set off in the car again.

'I'll just go and see what the Hallidays' villa is like,' Janey said, after a quick glance around the tiled ground floor with its little kitchenette and cane lounge furniture. Jean was already fiddling with the control for the air-con, so she slipped next door.

Alfie was sprawled across the large cane sofa as Mrs Halliday bustled around the kitchenette, making tea. 'Your father thought of everything, Janey,' she said, after checking that Mrs Brown wasn't behind her. 'Lady Grey tea, my favourite.'

'So where's the Spylab?' Janey didn't want to waste any time. As soon as her mum was asleep they could set off in search of Copernicus.

'Give us a break – we only just got here!' Alfie slipped off the sofa on to the tiles. 'Oooo, cooler down here.'

Mrs Halliday rattled some cups and saucers. 'I think Alfie's right for once, Janey. We should gather our strength, and make sure your mum's all settled in so she doesn't suspect anyth— oh! There you are, Jean. Cup of tea?'

Jean looked from one to the other of them. 'So she doesn't suspect what?'

She'd heard. Janey forced her jet-lagged brain to think of something, and quickly. 'Erm, Mrs Halliday just admitted that she knows the person who owns these villas, so we've got them really cheap.'

'Oh, but we can pay full price . . .' As Jean reacted in exactly the way Janey had known she would, the crisis was averted.

'If we don't have to, why should we?' Mrs Halliday passed Janey a cup of tea with a grateful look. 'They weren't booked for these two weeks, so we're doing them a favour, really.'

Janey's mum seemed satisfied with this. After a few slurps at her tea she put the cup down. 'I know I've just sat down for ten hours straight, but I'm suddenly exhausted. And it is midnight here after all. Janey, you and I are off to bed.'

'And so are we.' Mrs Halliday stifled a yawn. 'Then we can make the most of tomorrow.'

'Yeah. Can't wait to see Mickey Mouse,' said Alfie.

'Aww,' said Janey.

'I was joking. Du-uh.'

Laughing, Janey and her mum trotted back to their pale-green temporary home. She *was* actually very tired, Janey realized. With no Wower to revive her and keep her alert, sleep was upon her as soon as her head hit the cool linen pillow . . .

★

The sun streaming through the wooden blinds woke her after what seemed like only seconds. She could hear her mum having a shower, singing to herself, so Janey ambled downstairs and had a good look at their surroundings. There were no fireplaces, no cellars and no unexplained cupboards, so there was no obvious location for a Spylab, but Janey was pretty convinced there must be one around. It was already warm, so she stripped off the pyjamas that covered her golden SPIsuit and lifted her face and arms to the sun.

'And Janey Brown steps up to take her dive . . .' said a sarcastic voice somewhere above her head.

Alfie was leaning out of his bedroom window. 'Come down,' Janey said to him. 'It's really gorgeous.'

'We've got work to do, remember? Your dad sent this through,' he added in a whisper, dropping a piece of paper to the ground.

'As if I'd forget.' Janey stuck her tongue out at him as she scooped up the note, quickly turning it into a grin for her mother when Jean appeared in the doorway.

'Morning, darling,' said Jean, in a happy sing-song voice. 'Alfie, I thought we could all have breakfast together and work out what to do today. Ask your mum for me, will you?'

Alfie withdrew his head from the window and Jean put her arms around her daughter. 'Isn't this lovely? What a fabulous idea. I vote for Disney World today.'

'No, SeaWorld,' said Janey quickly. She had caught a quick glimpse of her father's note – a picture of an ear, followed by the SeaWorld logo – and knew *that* was where he wanted them to start their search for Copernicus. SeaWorld sounded like 'C' World, and it would be just like Copernicus, who was often referred to as The Big C, to turn a place full of sea creatures into CWorld.

'I want to go to SeaWorld,' she repeated.

'Sounds neat to me,' said Alfie, as he joined them for breakfast. He caught Janey's eye and winked.

'OK,' said Jean with a smile, fanning through tourist leaflets. 'We'll get a bus.'

'No need,' said Mrs Halliday, who had now appeared at the table. 'The chauffeur's at our disposal while we're here.'

'This really is the most incredible find.' Jean Brown gathered up her leaflets, shaking her head in pleased bewilderment, then went off to prepare herself for the day ahead.

Now that the spy team was alone, Mrs Halliday leaned in. 'That was a good bit of advice from your father. Looking for a squid in the ocean, even a mutant one, is a bit like looking for a needle in a haystack . . .'

'And SeaWorld is exactly the kind of place The

Big C would base his operations.' Janey nodded. 'Let's go.'

'Hang on,' said a voice from Janey's SPIV. 'First things first. Get your blonde behind to the villa vinivula . . . la.'

'The what?' said Janey.

Her SPI:KE tried again. 'The Villa Vanilla,' she intoned slowly. 'That's not easy to say.'

'Will do!' said Janey, and G-Mamma's face disappeared from view. Just then Janey caught sight of her mum coming back from their villa. 'Hey, Mum! Just realized I forgot my . . . er . . . hat! Back in a mo.'

Janey raced into their pistachio-coloured villa and pelted upstairs. The vanilla villa was next door, and she'd had an idea how to get inside it without being seen by her mum.

She flung open the French windows and ran out on to the little balcony. There was a matching one in all the villas, including the vanilla one . . .

Janey jumped as high as she could and smacked her feet against the balcony floor. *Bang!* With a familiar little explosion, her Four-Fs launched her into the air. Tucking her head under, Janey vaulted over her own balcony, somersaulted through the air and landed neatly on the Villa Vanilla balcony. She peered in the glass and the door swung open. 'Retinal recognition. Great!'

As Janey entered the Spylab that covered

37

the whole of the first floor of the villa, she heard an unmistakable 'miaow' – and her heart leaped. Trouble was here! G-Mamma must have Satispied him over to Florida! Janey gave him a quick stroke and a hug, then pointed to the cat flap at the bottom of the French windows. 'This is your home while we're here. Have a swim if you want, but don't act like you know us.'

The Spycat blinked his green eyes at her, taking in every word, then stalked off in search of further entertainment. As quickly as she could, Janey sprang back to her villa and ran out of the front door, grabbing her PERSPIRE on the way.

'Sorry, took ages to find it,' she explained breathlessly as her mother looked pointedly at her watch.

Jean glanced past her at something strolling along the line of the hedge. 'Good grief. Look at that cat – it's exactly like the one . . .'

'Let's go!' chorused Alfie, Mrs Halliday and Janey, and with a quick nod of his capped head Ronnie the chauffeur eased out through the gates and swung the car on to the highway.

It was very useful having a driver who knew his way around Orlando (and was probably armed with some useful SPI-buys, Janey guessed). Cooing over the wide boulevards, the palm trees and the melting blaze of sunshine, the Villa del Sol guests sat back in the car and enjoyed the ride. Within a short space of time they pulled up at the turnstiles ushering visitors into the exotic land of SeaWorld.

Alfie burst through the turnstile first, clutching his map. 'Look at all these white-knuckle rides! Yesss! Let's do Atlantis first.'

'Job to do, Alfie,' said Mrs Halliday in an under-tone, striding along behind him.

Janey crouched down and spread the park map on her lap. It really was a shame they were on a mission; there was so much to see – the mysterious manatees that sailors used to mistake for mermaids, the dolphins and seals who performed regularly throughout the day. But they had to focus, pick up on Copernicus's trail quickly. And as soon as Janey saw one particular word she knew where they ought to go.

'How about Shamu the *killer* whale?' she asked innocently.

Jean agreed readily as Alfie and his mother gave Janey an identical sharp-eyed look and then nodded. They set off across the park, traipsing through the blis-tering heat, and eventually arrived at Shamu's Happy Harbour.

'Shamu's show is in twenty minutes,' said Jean, studying the agenda. 'Let's see that and then think about getting some lunch. Or a drink at least. I'm exhausted already.'

Mrs Halliday was fanning herself with her handkerchief, also looking rather wilted; even Alfie was wiping his forehead and puffing loudly every few minutes. Janey was the only one standing up to the heat. The PERSPIRE must be keeping my head cool, she thought. They shuffled up to the ticket booth and took their seats around the pool while the arena filled up with tourists.

Suddenly there was a blast of music, and two keepers stepped out on to the platform beyond the pool, waving with both hands and smiling broadly. 'Welcome,' one of them called through his microphone, 'to Shamu's Happy Harbour!'

The crowd clapped and whooped, but then quietened down as the other keeper said, 'But it's not as happy as usual today, is it, Ben?'

'It's not, Jeremy. Shall we tell the audience why?'

Ben the keeper nodded and turned to the crowd. 'We've got a bit of sad news for ya. Shamu isn't feeling so good today.'

A disappointed 'Awww' rippled across the audience.

'That's right, Ben. We don't think Shamu can come out to play today.'

'Booooo,' called someone in the crowd. Jeremy and Ben suddenly grinned and turned to each other. 'D'ya hear that, Jeremy? I think our friends will be sad if they don't get some entertainment.'

Ben nodded as if he'd suddenly thought of something. 'Hey, how 'bout we bring out Helios instead?'

'We could do,' said Jeremy slowly. 'Whaddya think, guys? Should we bring out Helios, our brand-new killer whale?'

The odd person clapped and cheered, and then suddenly a chant filtered down from the back of the arena. 'Bring out Helios. Bring out Helios.'

'It's his first time . . .' warned Ben.

'Helios! Helios!'

Janey joined in, clapping her hands, but Alfie frowned. 'Helios?' he muttered. 'I think you'll find that's Greek for *sun*.'

Janey gasped as Helios appeared and arced through the air. The Sun King, she thought. That was one of the names that the power-mad Copernicus had bestowed upon himself.

The killer whale plunged back into the pool in a deluge that soaked all of the front three rows. Jean wiped her dripping face. 'Well, at least I feel a bit cooler now,' she said.

Jeremy and Ben belched out hearty laughs. 'Sorry, guys! You folks at the front might want to move back a little. Helios is coming right atcha!'

Janey's spy instincts tingled. A new killer whale – named for Copernicus, performing for the first time, on the very day that the spy team came to see the show? Interesting. Two minutes later, as she stared, terrified, into the open jaws of a killer whale, she knew just what her instincts had been trying to tell her.

dining with helios

Copernicus had trained this killer whale to kill Jane Blonde. And now Helios had launched himself right out of the pool, aiming straight for Janey's group. His terrifying, needle-teethed jaws were wide open. Janey was almost mesmerized by the cavernous depths of the whale's mouth.

And then she snapped into action.

'Out of the way!' She pushed her mother along the flooded bench where Jean collapsed in a bundle on the floor. Mrs Halliday rushed to her side, while in that instant Alfie and Janey upended the bench, aiming it inside the fast-approaching, murderous mouth. Helios's jaws snapped together in seconds, shattering the bench into splinters, but that gave Janey enough time to sprint past the whale, vault the tangled remains of the metal-and-perspex guard rail that was supposed to separate the whale from the audience and jump into the pool.

'Janey!' Alfie screamed, but Janey was only aware of one thing – she had to get rid of that whale before it got rid of her. Permanently. She glanced at the stands from the middle of the pool and was thrilled to see Helios floundering back to the water. She really was turning herself into fish bait.

Janey looked feverishly from side to side and then down.

She took a deep breath and turned turtle, diving for the bottom of the pool. As soon as she was out of sight, Janey grabbed her SPI Direct Energy Replenishment gadget from a concealed pocket in her gold SPIsuit and slipped the rubbery SPIder into her mouth. At least she could now breathe underwater. Helios must have entered the pool through some kind of gate, which probably led through to a holding pool. Maybe she could trap him in there? She swam away not a moment too soon as Helios sliced through the water towards her, hardly able to believe that his prey had leaped into his pool and was sitting on the bottom, practically asking to be eaten.

Janey waited until the whale drew near and opened its jaws again. At just the right moment she planted her feet against Helios's nose and bounced as hard as she could. Her Four-Fs detonated; Helios shot backwards, emitting a low, cow-like bellow. Janey rattled along the bottom of the pool. There was the gate! She raced up to it and clung to the close-set iron bars, but couldn't get through. She felt her way along the side of the pool, desperately aware that Helios had recovered himself and was once more headed straight for her. She had only moments. Was she going to get eaten? Or was she going to act like a Spylet? Die or spy, she thought grimly.

Then suddenly she saw it. An underwater window! Through it she could see some sort of restaurant and the words DINE WITH SHAMU written on an overhanging sign. The room was empty. Helios's black-and-red mouth loomed. With not a moment to spare, Janey wrenched off her left Four-F and looked for the button that would operate the circular saw. There! A tiny 'S' in a circle at the point at which the straps crossed over. She pressed. She prayed.

And she was flung backwards as the Four-F suddenly whizzed to life in her hand. Janey clung on to the strap and watched, amazed, as jagged saw-teeth appeared around the edge of the Four-F. She held it up to the glass, squinting just long enough to see in the reflective glass that the killer whale's jaws were practically upon her . . . there was a hideous shriek of metal on glass, then a line appeared down the middle of the window, and a million gallons of water pressed against the severed glass. It shattered outwards. Water sprayed and shards of tempered glass were blasted all over the dining tables. Janey was rushed along on a gushing torrent of water, straight out under the DINE

WITH SHAMU sign. When she turned around, Helios's nose was wedged tightly in the space where the window had been. She'd been very, very close to dining with Helios.

Janey was just picking herself up off the floor when her mother, Alfie and Mrs Halliday skidded into the room. 'Janey!' Jean Brown swept her up in an enormous embrace, while Alfie shouted, 'She's OK. She's down here,' to the very anxious Ben and Jeremy at the top of the stairs.

Ben wrung his hands, his face white with fear. 'We are so . . . so sorry! We've called for medical attention for you, and . . . Helios . . . We have to get him back in the other tank, and we will never, I repeat NEVER, again use a whale we haven't trained ourselves.'

'When did Helios arrive?' asked Mrs Halliday.

'His trainers brought him in a day or two ago – they said he'd been reared in captivity.'

'Well, you'd better make sure you have him safely locked up,' said Janey. 'And don't worry – it was just an accident. Could have happened to anyone.'

'NOT,' said Alfie under his breath.

The four of them slopped through the puddles and out of the restaurant. 'Are you sure you're all right, Janey?' asked her mum. 'You were underwater for so long. You might have suffered a lack of oxygen to your brain. How did that glass break? Why did you jump in the pool? Honestly, my heart nearly fell out of my mouth.' Jean kept up a stream of questions and statements of horror until they were once more out in the sunshine. 'What a bizarre, terrible thing to happen,' she said finally, making Janey sit down on a dolphin-shaped seat.

Funny how they always happen to me, thought Janey. She pulled her mum down next to her. 'I'm fine. I just . . . panicked and went the wrong way. But I'm not even hurt, honestly.'

She held up her gold-covered limbs for her mother to inspect, and finally Jean sat back, satisfied but still trembling. 'I definitely need a cup of tea now,' she said weakly.

It was exactly what the others needed – a chance to get back to the Spylab and report in to Abe. 'Good idea,' said Mrs Halliday. 'Let's go back to the villas and relax around the pool.'

All in agreement, they began the long walk back to the turnstiles and to Ronnie, who was waiting for them, as promised.

They collapsed gratefully into the air-conditioned car interior. 'That sun is just *melting*,' said Alfie, flopping out his tongue and panting like a dog.

'I've never been so hot,' agreed Mrs Halliday. 'Those last thirty metres were torture.'

Janey's mum propped her head up on her hand. 'Exhausted. Going to have to carry . . . a parasol.'

'What is wrong with you all?' Janey looked round

at them all from the seat beside Ronnie. 'I'm the one who just had a close encounter with a killer beast.'

But that didn't seem to matter. 'Tea,' said Mrs Halliday in a hoarse and longing whisper.

And tea it was, followed by a long lie-down by the pool, and more tea and cold lemonade in the mid-afternoon. Janey paced between the sun loungers, trying to motivate the others to do something – anything – more active, but nobody was interested. How could they just relax when Copernicus was obviously so close? They had to get on with finding him, with ensuring the safety of her dad's Revolution secret. Whatever his Revolution secret *was*. But it was no use. Frustrated, she went inside, then popped straight out of the French windows from the back bedroom, over the balcony and into the Villa Vanilla Spylab.

'Hey, Trouble,' she said, giving the cat a rub behind the ears. He was still a bit damp from having a paddle around the pool while they were out. Sitting down next to him at the workbench, Janey tapped into the computer and accessed G-Mamma.

'Blonde,' yelled her SPI:KE, 'give me the low-down.'

'I've just been attacked by a killer whale, and Copernicus is behind it,' she said matter-of-factly.

G-Mamma's round eyes doubled in size.

'Whopping whales, I'll let your boss man know immediately! In fact, I've just been talking

to your father.' G-Mamma leaned into the screen fur-
tively. 'He says Copernicus is behind the disappearance
of a few other animals from Solfari Lands. It's like he's
baiting your father, stealing from him so brazenly.'

'What kind of animals?' asked Janey.

'I don't want to say in case someone's listening in
with a SPI-Pod. But I'll act it out for you.' With that,
G-Mamma moved away from the screen so Janey
could see her in full. Then she pointed towards her
waist and mimed great surprise by making her eyes and
mouth very round.

'Er, sorry, I didn't get that.'

Again G-Mamma pointed towards her waist and
then looked very surprised.

'Waist . . . shock.' Janey shrugged. What on earth
could that mean?

'No! And don't say it out loud, Zany Janey.' Once
more she stuck out a finger and waved it at her waist,
but this time she let it come to rest just below her belt
and to the side.

'Ah!' Janey got it. Hip. But what was the other bit?
She watched G-Mamma's mouth go round and suddenly it came to her. Oh. Hip. Oh. Hippo. The animals
going missing were hippos!

'How many?' she said after giving G-Mamma a
thumbs-up to show she'd understood.

'Eleven. The entire stock.'

Janey thought for a moment. Monkeys missing,

hippos disappearing and killer whales attacking. What could it all mean? 'It's time we got to the bottom of this, G-Mamma. Dad's counting on us – but everyone's so jet-lagged at the moment, I feel like I'm on my own.'

'Well, not for long,' snapped G-Mamma as Janey left to rejoin the group by the pool.

G-Mamma was true to her word. An hour later, the Villa del Sol gates swung open and Ronnie nosed the car through. Janey, Alfie and their mothers all sat up to see what was going on just as a large figure in a florid, flouncy sundress clambered out of the front seat.

'It's me!' declared G-Mamma brightly. 'Goodness, what a coincidence. Fancy me and the kids landing in *exactly* the same holiday villas as you. We're in the coffee-coloured one, right?'

She pulled open the back door of the car. 'Come on, kids! Come and meet the neighbours.'

And to Janey's great astonishment two children stepped sheepishly from the car: Tish, in a red SPIsuit like Janey's, and Leaf, in green board shorts and rash shirt like Alfie's.

G-Mamma beamed. 'Oh, aren't we all going to have FUN! Now, did I see a teapot?'

Having thrown back a flagon of tea, G-Mamma installed herself and her two Spylets in the coffee-coloured villa while Jean Brown hissed questions at Janey.

'How on earth did that mad woman from next door end up here? Whose children are those? Did you hear them? They don't even have the same accents. Do you think we should alert the authorities? And where did she find that dress?'

Janey held up her hands as if in defeat. How could she explain it all to her mum?

'Rosie Biggenham!' said Mrs Halliday, stepping into the breach. 'Fancy her turning up like that. She used to be a teacher at one of my old schools, you know, Jean. The kids all loved her – she left to start fostering children. Those must be two of her foster children, back with her for a holiday. Very big . . . um . . . heart that woman has.'

Alfie headed off for a dip in the pool, hissing, 'Very big *everything*.'

Jean Brown shook her head, blinking rapidly. 'Well, to be honest I see quite enough of her at home, without her turning up on our holiday like this. I'm sure she's very nice and everything . . .'

'She is very nice,' said Janey. 'You should try to get to know her a bit more.' And I should be able to get on with my mission, now that I've got some more back-up, she thought.

But Janey was sadly disappointed. The new arrivals

emerged from the coffee-coloured villa in their sun and swimming gear, G-Mamma sporting a large floral swimming cap that made her head look like a sea anemone. Grabbing a lounger each, they stretched out to have a chat with their new neighbours, tipping suncream over themselves, only for Janey to find that the conversation had stopped within fifteen minutes. Everyone except Leaf had dropped off and lay sprawled out like cats in the sunshine. 'I know we're meant to relax,' she said softly to Leaf as she looked at the sleeping forms around them, 'but this is just pathetic.'

He shrugged. 'They are just not used to sun this strong. Where I come from, in the summer it is bright sunshine until three o'clock in the morning, so I am very used to it.'

'Well, I'm not,' said Janey, 'but I seem to be OK.'

'They are just not as strong as we are, Blonde,' said Leaf. 'Volleyball?'

The Spylets batted a ball around in the pool while Leaf explained that they had gathered their spygear together as soon as Janey had spoken with G-Mamma, and then had Satispied over to the Florida Spylab. Then they'd had to sneak out the back of the villa, climb into the car and make their official entrance through the front gate. 'Father is still working with Mr Rownigan on this Revolution process, and we have left the protection of Solfari Lands to the Bird family.'

'Is that safe?' said Janey, who still couldn't fully trust Blackbird.

Leaf shrugged. 'How much of this is ever safe?'

'True.' Leaf was right. Theirs was not a safe world. And she'd dragged her mum right into the middle of it. Blackbird was definitely not the only one who made 'errors of judgement'.

As twilight fell, the two Spylets finally managed to wake up the other members of their party, and they all sat around the barbecue trying to make polite conversation while Mrs Halliday and Alfie assembled hot dogs and passed them around.

'One or two?' said Mrs Halliday to Tish.

'Four, please,' called G-Mamma before Tish had a chance to open her mouth. 'All that travelling has worn me out. In fact,' she said with a gigantic yawn that rather reminded Janey of being chased around the pool by Helios, 'I must have jet lag. Straight to bed after this snack.'

Straight to bed. Janey almost smirked. G-Mamma was making an excuse, covering for them so that they could all get off to bed early, meet up in the Spylab and begin a serious search-and-destroy campaign on Copernicus. A little thrill ran through her; soon the mission would be properly underway.

G-Mamma was as good as her word. As soon as the last onion shred had been scooped off the plate, she nodded at Tish and Leaf. 'Beddy bye-byes for weary travellers. Come on, kidlets – you snooze or you lose.'

Janey stood up quickly.

'Me too!' she stretched her arms. 'I'm pretty tired – didn't have a long nap like the rest of you. I think I'll go up to bed as well.'

Everybody else levered themselves off their chairs at the same time. 'I'm still quite tired,' said Jean, rubbing her eyes.

'Yes, today was quite . . . challenging,' agreed Mrs Halliday. 'We can wash up in the morning.'

Alfie stared. 'Are you feeling all right?' he said to his mother. 'We never leave the washing up.'

But Mrs Halliday just waved her hand. 'We're on holiday, Alfie. I can't summon up the energy to care about it.'

They all said goodnight and sloped off to their respective villas. Janey hopped around in her room until she was sure her mother would be asleep, then sneaked out on the balcony to vault across to the Spylab. Apart from Trouble cleaning his paws on the computer bench, the place was completely empty. To fill the time while she waited for the others, Janey chatted to Trouble as she stroked his tawny head before sending him into the Wower. 'We're off on a mission,' she told him as she stowed a fresh SPIder in her pocket, got her new ASPIC ready and added a golden Girl-gauntlet to her summer SPIsuit. After twenty minutes, however, there was still no sign of anyone else.

With a sigh, Janey Four-F'd her way across the back balconies to get to Alfie's room. Through the French windows she could see him sprawled at an angle across the bed; it looked as though he'd barely made it into the room before collapsing.

'Alfie!' Janey tapped on the window. 'Wake up!'

He didn't stir, so she moved along the balcony to the next windows. 'Holidays are bad for spies,' Janey whispered to Trouble. 'They just relax too much.' Mrs Halliday was also fast asleep, and no amount of door rattling was going to wake her.

The picture was very much the same at G-Mamma's. It looked as though the SPI:KE had fallen asleep halfway through taking off her make-up, spread-eagled at the dressing table. Janey knocked on the glass. 'G-Mamma!' There was a brief snort as G-Mamma shifted in her seat, but that was all.

Janey had had enough. 'Trouble, sabre-claw your way through this window,' she instructed, pointing to the little pane of glass directly below the door handle. Trouble didn't need to be asked twice, and he flicked open the biggest claw on his front paw. It curved towards the door like a pirate's cutlass, and in seconds Trouble had stripped out the putty holding in the glass so the pane dropped out in one piece on to Janey's out-stretched, Girl-gauntlet-protected hand.

Janey ran to G-Mamma's side. 'Wake up,' she said urgently, shaking her SPI:KE's shoulder. 'Come on!' Nothing seemed to stir her. Janey changed tack and crooned directly into G-Mamma's ear. 'I've got doughnuts.'

G-Mamma sat up with a start, one eye still surrounded with Perfect Purple eye-dazzle, the other clean, small and beady. For a second Janey was reminded of Copernicus's mismatched eyes – one human, one yellow and monstrous. 'Whaddya . . . where?' said G-Mamma blearily.

'Come on,' said Janey. 'We've got to track down Copernicus.'

'Does he have the doughnuts?'

Janey nearly stamped her foot with frustration as her SPIK:E's eyes closed again.

It was no use. Janey couldn't believe it. Another night wasted. 'Perfect,' she said bitterly. 'On my own again.'

Except I'm not, thought Janey as she logged into the Spylab computer. Her dad would know what to do. It was time to ask him directly. Then tomorrow she'd be able to start the search – with or without help.

the river
of grass

'Do I look like a hippo-hunter?' G-Mamma yawned.

Janey looked at the tired faces grouped around the Spylab. She'd managed to wake the team at dawn after she'd received an email from her dad. He wanted them to locate the missing hippos – immediately. 'My dad said we have to,' she told them firmly. 'Find a river, find the hippos.' It was a clear directive and the snoozing spies were not going to wriggle out of it.

Once the grumbling spy team had agreed to meet for breakfast in five minutes, Janey jumped over the balcony and into her bedroom just as she heard her mum come out of her bedroom.

'Up already?' Jean's tousled head appeared around the door. 'Janey, I think you should change out of that gold swimsuit thing. And take that hat off. You've been wearing them non-stop since we set off.'

Janey looked down at her SPIsuit. 'But . . . it's really

comfy,' she said pleadingly. 'And I do keep swimming in it, so it's clean and everything.'

'You know, I'm just wondering,' said her mother, staring at Janey's golden outfit, 'where you got it from anyway. I don't remember buying it for you.'

'Mrs Halliday got it when she bought Alfie's swimming stuff.' Janey smiled to cover up yet another lie she had told her mother. Inwardly she sighed. It would be so nice to be able to tell her the truth.

'OK,' said Jean. 'Well, let's see if Mad Rosie's managed breakfast this morning.'

'Oh, I'm sure she has.'

Janey pushed her mum ahead of her along the landing, and together they made their way out into the bright morning sunshine. It was already warm, and G-Mamma was glowing as she flipped fried eggs on the barbecue griddle. 'Sunny side up,' she carolled as Janey took a plate. 'Just right for Florida. Although, jeepers, it's hot! Next time I do breakfast we're having ice cream.'

'So what's the plan?' Jean added some bacon to her plate of eggs and sat down at the large wooden table, adding hopefully, 'Disney World maybe?'

The group hummed and hawed reluctantly. 'I think it may be a bit hot to walk around another theme park,' said Mrs Halliday.

'I vote for somewhere natural,' said Leaf.

Tish nodded enthusiastically. 'Oh, I love . . .

natural things. How about somewhere with a . . . I don't know . . . a river?'

'Sounds good to me,' said Alfie quickly.

'Great idea!' said Janey, who was quickly scanning through her mum's collection of tourist-attraction leaflets. 'Let's go to the Everglades!' she shouted a little too loudly, as she flicked past one particular leaflet. 'It's meant to be really interesting, Mum,' she added more quietly.

Everyone agreed that the Everglades would be perfect and very soon the chauffeur-driven car pulled into the driveway. Ronnie got out of the car, mopping his brow with a great yellow handkerchief. 'Where to today, folks?' he said breathlessly.

'The Everglades, please,' said Janey eagerly.

Ronnie's chubby face stretched into a smile. 'Ah, the River of Grass,' he said with a slow nod. 'You'll have a lot of fun there. Just watch out for gators.'

'What are gators?' Tish asked as she climbed into the very back seat with Leaf and Alfie.

Ronnie held the door as Janey, her mum and Mrs Halliday got into the middle seat and G-Mamma eased herself into the passenger seat next to the driver. 'You'll see,' he said with a grin. 'It's a real long drive, so I'll take you to the airport instead and we'll fly there. All courtesy of Villa del Sol.'

Half an hour later they were boarding a small plane that bobbed on a little lake near the tiny airport.

Janey glanced at the two floats beneath the fuselage. She suspected it was the same plane that had brought them from home, only with a few additions and extra gadgetry, and she saw her mother look along its length with a puzzled expression.

'Cool!' said Alfie breathlessly.

'This holiday package is just . . . unbelievable,' Jean Brown muttered.

Janey squeezed her arm. 'Are you having a good time, Mum?'

'The best!' Jean gave her a thumbs-up. 'Even with Dozy Rosie from next door.' And she smiled happily as she buckled her seat belt.

The plane ride was uneventful, apart from a small loop-the-loop when an ecstatic Alfie was invited to take the controls by Ronnie – who it turned out was a pilot as well as a driver – and soon they were landing on a wide and murky river among the lush greenery of the Everglades.

'I am seeing why they call it the River of Grass,' said Leaf, almost disappearing from view as they disembarked on to a narrow walkway and his green SPIsuit blended with the vegetation.

'Keep your toes away from the edge,' called Ronnie from the front of the line. 'We don't want those gators to have them.'

Janey looked down at the water and, sure enough, a knobbly, sinuous body was slipping away from the walkway into the reeds. Not gators. Alligators. She definitely planned on staying out of *their* way . . .

Ronnie took the lead, pointing out various features. Then, as they reached a gate to a small enclosure, he stopped suddenly. 'Sorry, folks, just got a bit hot and bothered there,' he panted. 'That's better . . . and here's your next method of transportation.'

He pointed over the gate to a strange contraption parked at the riverside. It looked rather like a small stage with a cage at the back, balanced high above some enormous inflated tank tyres.

Alfie drew in a sharp breath, like a backwards sigh. 'Swamp buggy,' he crooned, hardly able to speak. 'Pontoon bodywork, racing engine, big flat flotation tyres, paddle treads on the rear for the forward motion, rudder steering . . .'

He stumbled over the flattened grass towards the vehicle, but G-Mamma swiped him across the head with her large floral PERSPIRE. 'Oi, Petrolhead!' she barked. 'Ladies first.'

The swamp buggy rocked dangerously as G-Mamma climbed aboard, helped by Ronnie, then the others slotted themselves into the seats that were bolted to the floor. 'Strap yourselves in and hold tight!' yelled Ronnie.

The engine whined, spluttered into action and then burst into life with a roar like a caged animal released from its prison. Janey clutched Alfie's arm as they skated across the surface of the river at forty miles an hour, flattening reeds and shooting out a frothy wake like milkshake.

'I have got to get one of these!' said Alfie, his face radiant with joy.

Janey took in as much as she could while Ronnie whipped them around the river, screaming as if they were on a roller coaster. It certainly looked tropical enough for hippos. Suddenly the engine note changed and the buggy slowed down.

'We're right in the heart of gator land now,' said Ronnie softly, bringing the swamp buggy to a stop for a moment. 'Look around, folks.'

They all did as they were told. At first the river looked uninhabited, calm even, but then Ronnie tossed a lump of meat over the side and the water below them began to boil. One, two . . . many sets of long, evil-teethed jaws broke the surface, like monstrous baby birds snapping for food, and all around, glinting in the sunlight that danced through the treetops, was a writhing, thrashing mass of reptilian killers. One even managed to reach up to the edge of the platform, snapping ferociously. Janey stared in horror at the long, clawed foot, so like a deformed human hand . . .

G-Mamma leaned forward and hissed in Janey's ear: 'Compared with this lot, old Copper Knickers is a pussycat! I think I'm a gator-hater.'

Janey just nodded, then she glanced back at Ronnie, urging him to move on. The sweat was running off his forehead and down his cheeks, but after wiping his face on his sleeve he revved up the engine again. 'That sun's a scorcher,' he said, 'even through the trees. Let's head for one of the camps and grab ourselves some lunch.'

'Before something grabs *us* for lunch,' said Tish with a cheery, gap-toothed grin.

The sun beat down on them as they found their way to the picnic tables, safely fenced off from the riverbank with the odd cypress tree creating scant shade. Everyone fell upon the picnic with gusto, tearing into the fried chicken legs and great chunky sandwiches with as much fervor as the alligators had greeted the meat. The meal was rounded off with more doughnuts than even G-Mamma could manage and washed down with gallons of fresh, cool water.

Jean stretched. 'That was lovely. Funny how it's so relaxing even with those alligators so close by.'

'It's a real holiday, isn't it, Jean?' agreed Mrs Halliday, lying down full length on one of the blankets they'd spread on the ground. 'I could do with a nap.'

Ronnie looked delighted. 'If you folks all want a siesta, that's fine by me. This heat's got me beat today.'

'Sticky buns, sweaty suns . . . heat's got me beat . . .' yawned G-Mamma. 'I'd make up a rap if I had the energy. Hmm, sticky bu—'

She stopped abruptly. Janey couldn't believe it: G-Mamma had simply fallen asleep. Alfie had been sketching swamp buggies on his napkin, but his head was now nodding towards the table. 'Five minutes,' he mumbled incoherently. 'Power nap . . .' Everyone had decided to take full advantage of siesta time, apart from Leaf, who was packing up the picnic hamper.

Well, Janey wasn't going to waste any more time. She had a plan. 'I'm going to take another look around,' she said to Leaf.

His eyes followed hers down to the riverbank. 'Take care,' he said. 'I will keep lookout for everyone here.'

Janey grabbed some meat from a bag and approached the edge of the river cautiously.

'OK, gators, let's get you out of the way,' she whispered, before lobbing the meat towards the far bank of the river as far away as she could. Almost instantly, three or four alligators emerged from the water, lured by the scent of the blood, and swam away from Janey. She made her way carefully into the reeds, looking for clues of some kind. Hippo poo? She wouldn't be able to tell it from alligator poo. She'd been searching for over half an hour before she came across something that might be significant.

It was a footprint: a wide, splayed, four-toed impression the size of a dinner plate. Janey studied it carefully. It certainly didn't look like a print made by the shrivelled claw of an alligator . . .

Then she remembered a way she could find out. She took off her PERSPIRE, turned it over and pressed the tiny button at the centre of the cap.

Instantly a touch-screen keyboard was projected on to the underside of the cap's peak, and the inside glowed white like a ghostly television screen. 'OK.' Janey typed in the words 'hippo foot' and waited.

An image popped up on to the screen – a four-toed foot, with toes splayed left and right and two facing forward. She looked at the footprint next to her. It was an exact match.

'Where do hippos live?' she tapped in next.

'"Hippos are found in sub-Saharan Africa",' she read, '"where they are largely considered to be the most dangerous wild animal of all, weighing up to 3,600 kilograms and capable of running at speeds of twenty miles an hour."' Janey glanced at her Fleet-Feet-Flip-flops. 'Well, I'm faster than that.'

She popped her PERSPIRE back on and returned to the picnic area where Leaf, still the only one awake, was whittling a piece of wood into the shape of an alligator.

'Dad was right,' said Janey quietly, straining to be heard above the cacophony of snorts and snores that filled the air. 'There are hippos here, and they aren't usually found living in the wild in America.'

Leaf looked around at their sleeping companions. He shrugged. 'There is not much we can do at the moment.'

But Jane Blonde wasn't used to waiting when there was a mission at hand. 'There is something we can do. Cover for me,' she said, and took off into the thickly knotted mangroves.

terrifying teeth

Janey found her way back to the hippopotamus foot-print, hoping to find another – a neat, obliging little trail of prints that would lead her directly to the stolen hippos. What she did find was rather more alarming: two sets of claw marks, raked into the mud, with a sweep of mud between them. An alligator had been on this bank since her last visit and had slid back into the water, perhaps even dragging a hippo with it. And if it could drag a hippo, it could certainly topple Jane Blonde. Topple her, seize her in its jaws and crunch her to Blonde-dust. She had to be quick.

Janey scanned the area. 'Where are they?' she muttered.

Suddenly she thought of something – a way to find the footprints easily without having to rummage around in the alligator-infested mangroves looking for them. Pulling off her PERSPIRE, she brought up the image of the four-toed hippo print, then focused her

Ultra-gogs on it. 'Match,' she said firmly. 'Match and find.'

She put her hat back on and turned slowly on the spot, allowing her Ultra-gogs to scan the area for footprints. Suddenly her spy glasses gave a beep and zoomed in on an image. Janey examined it excitedly. 'It worked!' she cried. 'And again. Match and find.'

As she scanned further along the bank, the Ultra-gogs whirred, clicked into focus and then emitted a loud *BEEEEP*.

'Perfect!' Janey slithered along to the next footprint. It was still only a single print, but if the Ultra-gogs could keep 'matching and finding', she'd be bound to come across a whole hippo soon . . .

She lurched from one footprint to the next. Occasionally she would find two prints and imagine hopefully that the hippo was just beyond the next mangrove tree, only to find the next print half submerged in water much further on.

Eventually, as Janey looked upwards for the first time and noticed that it was getting dark, she started to feel worried. Perhaps she was never going to find this hippo. Maybe someone – some enemy spy – had laid a trail for her and was luring her further and further away from her spy team. She looked back the way she had come, and her heart sank. How far had she travelled? What if she got lost?

'Match and find,' said Janey once more,

trying to gather her courage by focusing on the job in hand.

She turned her head this way and that, waiting, hoping for the bright *BEEP* that signified a new foot-print. But the Ultra-gogs were completely silent. And then Janey saw them.

Four alligators were swinging their monstrous bodies through the mangroves, their flat heads parting the grasses like chainsaws, evil green-gold eyes glowing in the gathering gloom. The colour of their skin was so mud-like that were it not for the glint of their eyes, Janey would hardly have seen them . . .

Then they opened their mouths, and Janey real-ized the beasts were moving in for the kill. For a moment she was too stunned to do anything. Then she jumped.

Flinging herself up in the air, Janey brought her knees up to her chest and slammed her feet back down against the ground, hoping that she wouldn't slip in the mud and deliver herself into the nearest cavernous mouth. Her feet made contact only briefly, and she staggered slightly as the Four-Fs detonated beneath her and launched her towards the sky like a firework.

Unfortunately, her slight stumble at take-off meant that she'd been launched at an angle, an angle that had directed her away from the bank towards the murky middle of the river.

'Oh no,' said Janey. She had no Girl-gauntlet, no

ASPIC – in fact, no way of escaping the alligators' jaws of death as she fell into the Everglades. And she'd brought it all on herself, assuming once more that Jane Blonde, even on her own, could do anything.

The water rushed up to meet her, her feet hit the surface . . .

And stayed there.

She opened her eyes. I'm walking on water, she thought.

Janey couldn't believe what she was seeing – it was a miracle. She seemed to be standing on something solid, yet she could feel water all around her feet. Meanwhile, the alligators had noticed that their supper was standing only metres away from them; with a flick of their loathsome tails they headed straight for her.

Janey ran, her feet splashing as quickly across the surface as her Four-Fs would allow her. It felt like she was leaping across a strange causeway until, with a sob of relief, she hit dry land on the far riverbank.

'Zoom,' she said, her heart beating wildly. The alligators had not given chase – but something was close by. An eye blinked malevolently from the water, reflecting the shimmer from the rising moon. Janey zoomed in once more with her Ultra-gogs. To her astonishment a round ear, rather like a teddy bear's but without the fur, had risen up above the water near the eye. Then she spotted another set of eyes . . . and another.

Janey swallowed hard as the nearest pair of

eyes moved closer. She peered into the water, hardly able to believe what she was seeing.

The causeway she had run across was breaking up. Parts were paddling downstream, while other bits of it were lining up and approaching the riverbank. Fast. She hadn't been walking on water after all. Jane Blonde had simply had the good luck to land on the back of a submerged hippopotamus and had run right across the river on a walkway of hippos, lurking just under the surface of the water.

But now they were coming for her. What was it the PERSPIRE had told her? Hippos were known as the most dangerous African animal? They looked so cute at the zoo, but as one clambered purposefully out of the water, lowered its head and opened its enormous mouth wide, Janey suddenly remembered the rest of the information. They weighed 3,600 kilograms, and ran at twenty miles an hour. She was about to be chased by . . . she counted quickly . . . eleven of the world's most deadly animals. Then, just as she felt the ground shudder beneath the weight of the attacking hippos, Janey heard a sound that lifted her heart – a splutter and a roar of engines, then the cry of her best friend and fellow Spylet: 'Blonde! Get ready to jump!'

The swamp buggy blasted around the bend through the gathering darkness, lights blazing and engine roaring. Tish and Leaf were leaning off the front of the buggy, Girl-gauntlet and Boy-battler at the ready. Alfie, meanwhile, was hanging on to the rudder with both hands, zig-zagging across the river.

'Three . . .' he hollered so loudly that Janey realized he must be shouting into the MIC setting on his SPI-Pod. 'Two . . .' The buggy swerved into its final lunge towards Janey. 'One . . . NOW.'

Just as the swamp buggy slid sideways towards her, two more hippo heads emerged from the water. Taking off from the slippery riverbank, she planted a foot on each head, right between the teddy-like ears, and vaulted off them towards the boat. Tish and Leaf each reached out to grab one of her hands, and in the next second Janey was lying in a crumpled pile between the buggy's seats.

'Blonde!' Alfie pulled away, dodging hippos and alligators. His face was alight with joy and excitement.

'What?' asked Janey, who was more than a little dazed.

'This baby,' he said, patting the rudder beneath his hand, 'drives like an absolute *dream*.'

Janey rolled her eyes. 'Right,' she said. 'Nice to see you too.'

tired old tiger

They arrived back at the Villa del Sol sometime after midnight, Janey holding her mother's hand all the way. Jean had woken up to find her daughter had disappeared; convinced she had been dragged away by alligators, she had screamed so loudly that everyone woke up. Leaf quickly explained that Janey had just gone to the toilet, and when Tish and Alfie had realized what was going on, they insisted that they needed to go too. The Spylets had made straight for Ronnie's swamp buggy. While they were gone, Mrs Halliday and G-Mamma calmly packed the picnic gear and fielded Jean Brown's questions.

Now Janey wished for the millionth time since she'd become a Spylet that she could just tell her mother the truth. Instead she settled for making sure Jean was asleep, then getting across to the Spylab and telling the others about her discoveries.

'They were all there,' she said to the assembled

SPI:KEs and Spylets. 'Eleven hippos, just lying around in the Everglades.'

'I know how they felt,' said G-Mamma, her eye make-up smudged after her afternoon-long nap.

'You have to fight the heat,' said Janey. 'You have to keep going.'

'You're right, Janey,' said Mrs Halliday. 'But right now it's night-time and we're all a bit more alert. What's our plan?'

Tish stuck up her hand. 'How about Satispying back to the Everglades, rounding up those hippos and sending them back to Solfari Lands?'

Leaf apparently agreed. 'I volunteer to go back to the Everglades tonight.'

'I'll come with you.' Janey pulled a Girl-gauntlet from a cupboard. She wasn't going without full protection this time.

'Me too,' said G-Mamma. 'And Tish, seeing as it was her idea.'

It was agreed that they would be the hippo party, while Alfie and Mrs Halliday would watch out for Jean Brown, alert Abe Rownigan and operate the Satispy remote control. Seconds later, the three Spylets zapped down in the swamp, a traffic light of red, gold and green SPIsuits, followed by G-Mamma in shimmering grey. When she shoved a SPIder in her mouth and lowered herself under the water, she looked rather like a hippo herself. 'Come on

. . . bloop burple,' she called as her mouth filled with water, waggling her eyebrows to encourage the others to follow.

They submerged themselves, Ultra-gogs on both night and water vision, gloves at the ready to fight off any passing alligators or persuade any hippos who were less than keen to go back to the zoo.

After a few minutes of groping around in the murky river the Spylets and SPI:KE popped up above the surface. 'Nothing,' said Janey. 'But they were all here. Honestly.'

Leaf nodded. 'We saw them too. How about I get that swamp buggy and we check a bit further . . .'

'Forget it, Leafo,' snapped G-Mamma. 'It's my turn with the boys' toys. Blonde, you come with me. Titian and Leaf, you make for those cypress trees. Any trouble, SPIV me.'

Leaf merely raised an eyebrow, popped his SPIder back in his mouth and followed Tish, who was already cutting through the water in a steady and rather impressive front crawl. Janey and her SPI:KE climbed aboard the swamp buggy and blasted off in the other direction, slewing to a halt at intervals so Janey could bob into the water and have a look beneath the surface. Every so often they caught sight of an alligator's tail or a pair of glowing amber eyes, but it became very evident, after several miles had been covered, that the hippos were no longer there.

'Mud, mud, glorious mud,' sang G-Mamma quietly. 'Nothing quite like it for disguising missing hippos . . . So follow me, follow, down to the hollow, and there let us wallow, because there's absolutely noooooooothing else there . . .'

Janey shrugged her shoulders where the rising sun was beginning to warm them. 'This is hopeless. They've been moved. Copernicus must have found out we were on to them.'

At that moment the SPIV around her neck buzzed into life. Leaf's face appeared, smothering a yawn. 'There is nothing here. We are back at the picnic place, and we have seen a couple of alligators, but that is all.' He panned the SPIV around the picnic site to demonstrate. It was completely quiet, apart from the gentle sound of Tish snoring, curled up on a picnic bench. 'We are both very exhausted,' Leaf explained. 'All that swimming . . .'

G-Mamma's head was also starting to loll so Janey grabbed the rudder and turned them around. 'We'll head back to the site,' she told Leaf. 'We might as well go home.'

They Satispied back to the familiar welcome of the Villa del Sol. Mrs Halliday and Alfie passed the details on to Solfari Lands after a brief decode and debrief session. Janey stood under the spy shower, letting the incredible droplets melt away a hard night's spy work. Leaf, Tish and G-Mamma, meanwhile, had simply collapsed on the sunbeds outside their villa and fallen asleep.

An hour later Jean Brown got up from the breakfast table and angled a parasol over G-Mamma's face. 'She's starting to look like a pumpkin.'

'Ugh,' snorted Alfie. 'Imagine that all carved out with a candle in it. Very Halloween.'

'That's enough.' Mrs Halliday pushed her croissant to one side. 'In fact, I think a little dozing in the sun looks like a very good idea. We'll just hang around here today, I think.'

To Janey's surprise, Alfie didn't argue but simply nodded and yawned. At least now I can get to Disney World with Mum, thought Janey. Even Spylets need a day off.

Jean Brown was delighted with the suggestion. 'Yes! Great idea, Janey.'

Janey, now in shorts and a strappy T-shirt, was soon jumping into the back of the car, and as the ever-obliging Ronnie drove them up to the turnstiles of the Magic Kingdom, her mum jiggled up and down on her seat. 'I'm so excited!' she said, beaming.

Janey smiled. If only Jean knew how exciting her own spy life used to be.

The theme park was tremendous fun. They queued for thrilling rides, waved at various characters and watched scenes from films re-enacted before their very eyes. By lunchtime Janey was exhausted, and even Jean's enthusiasm seemed to have dwindled. She sank on to a stone toadstool, fanning herself with the guidebook.

'Gosh, it's hot. I might have to go back to the villa for a swim,' she said, sweat trickling from the browband of her hat.

Janey had to agree. All her clothes were sticking to her in a way that her golden SPIsuit never did, and a crushing headache gripped her brain so that planning the next event seemed too difficult a task. She peered at the guide. 'The parade's at three. Why don't we sit in the shade until then?'

Her mum agreed, and together they staggered to a refreshment site. Many other people had had the same idea, and the queues for drinks and ice creams were bigger than some of the queues for the rides. A nice family from Germany took pity on the Browns and allowed them to perch on the end of their shaded table, and Jean revived enough to get food and water for them both.

Janey smiled at the family – mum, dad and two boys about seven years old – as her mum headed towards the counter, banging into tables as she went. 'Hot,' she said, fanning her face.

'*Ja!*' said the mother, pointing to her children. One of the boys was crying listlessly into his fries, and the other was slumped against his father, who had his head propped in his hands as he slurped his supersize cola.

Looking around, Janey could see that everyone was feeling the same way. A family a few tables away was bickering over a water bottle, and a small tussle broke out between the mother and her teenage daughter. Elsewhere people were quiet, sticking out their lower lips to blow cooling air over their sticky faces, or fanning themselves with whatever they could get their hands on.

Finally, Jean Brown came back with their lunch. 'That was hard work,' she said breathlessly. 'One of the staff had passed out behind the counter, and the others were just stepping over him, they were so busy.'

'This is mad, Mum,' said Janey, stifling an enormous yawn. 'Why don't we just forget the parade?'

'I want to see Mickey Mouse,' said her mother firmly. 'And Pooh Bear.'

'OK,' said Janey with a grin. Deep down she really wanted to see them too. And by the time they had finished their salads and bottles of water, and had had a little snooze in their seats, it was almost three o'clock anyway . . .

They lined up with what felt like the rest of America, with hundreds of fractious children and equally ratty adults. There was a lacklustre cheer as the parade began, and Jean Brown turned a yawn into a grin. 'The Little Mermaid!' she cried, nudging Janey. 'She used to be your favourite. And Cinderella. And . . . what's that one called?' She stopped, puzzled.

'Snow White,' said Janey.

Jean shook herself. 'Snow White! How could I forget that? It's so hot out here I can hardly think.'

She wasn't the only one, it seemed. Janey peered more closely as the elaborately decorated float with the Little Mermaid on it passed by. The mermaid was asleep, statue-like, with her hand in a wave and her head tipped to one side. The other characters were just managing to shuffle along, nodding to the crowd, or perhaps nodding with fatigue, and then Janey spotted her mum's favourite further along the parade.

'Look, Mum,' she said. 'It's Tigger!'

They both turned in delight, but their expressions turned to horrified bafflement as the famous tiger raised his right paw, tottered for a moment as if he'd lifted something heavy over his head, then careered with little stumbling steps straight into the crowd.

'Get his costume off,' shouted one of the more alert onlookers, a man in a bright yellow shirt.

'No! You'll spoil the magic for the children.' His wife gave his arm a slap.

'But he'll suffocate!' The man wrestled with Tigger's head. 'I think that might ruin the magic too.'

And when Tigger's head came off to reveal a red-faced teenage girl, yelling, 'No, Mom.

I don't want to get up yet!' Janey turned to her mother.

'Mum, I'm really tired. Shall we go now?'

To her relief, her mum nodded. 'I need a dip.'

Ronnie whacked the air-conditioning on full and cruised along to the villas where they'd planned on getting the others together. It was not as easy as they'd thought. Every one of Janey's spy team was flat out and snoring by the pool. They hadn't moved since that morning. Janey shook Mrs Halliday.

'Mrs H,' she said. 'we're going for a swim in the sea. Do you want to come?'

Mrs Halliday sat up blearily. 'Sharks!' she shouted, then lay down again.

Janey tried Alfie instead. 'Come on, Al. You can try the surf. Let's go.'

'Five minutes,' he groaned, holding up three fingers.

Only Leaf responded quickly. 'What is the problem?' He sat up with a start and Janey explained that they were off for a swim in the ocean. 'Ah yes. That is a good idea. I will help you wake the others.' And with that he ran up to the small diving board and launched himself into the pool.

'Whazzat?' G-Mamma sat bolt upright, one of her false eyelashes stuck to her cheek. She patted her damp legs. 'Whysitallwet? Whatsssgoingon? Stopitlittlegreenboy.'

Leaf grinned and dive-bombed the pool again. Within moments the resulting splash had roused everybody. 'Come on, you lot,' pleaded Janey. 'A swim will wake you up.'

Alfie groaned, but he still gathered up his surfboard and headed for the car.

The others followed reluctantly after taking quick Wowers to get into their SPIsuit surf gear. Ronnie held the boot open casually, so that Trouble could jump in, and soon they were speeding along towards the coast, the air-conditioning raising their spirits as it lowered their temperatures.

The beach looked stunning in the glorious sunlight, as though a sunbeam had been captured and stretched along the coast. Janey pulled her PERSPIRE down over her eyes. All around them, the sand was littered with sleeping bodies in varying shades of sunburn; the spies and Mrs Brown piled their clothes under a sun umbrella and plunged into the sea.

'Do those sunbathers know something we don't?' Jean looked around as they ploughed through the waves. They were the only ones in the water.

Janey glanced back towards the beach but said nothing. The cool water was such bliss that she wasn't about to mention to Jean that the waves might be home to a rare mutant Colossal Squid. Back on the sand there was only one upright figure – a little boy, watching them solemnly with his arms wrapped around his knees. Behind him, Ronnie leaned on the car, fanning himself and occasionally scratching Trouble's head. 'I think they're all just asleep. Come on, we'll be fine.'

For half an hour they splashed and played in the surf, the adults bobbing in cool bliss, the Spylets body-surfing and dunking each other, gradually getting deeper and deeper and allowing the cool water to wake them up thoroughly.

This is fun, thought Janey. Just like a real, normal holiday, doing real things with normal people – well, normalish people. And she allowed herself to cast off the burden of Spylet and concentrate on being a girl: a girl playing with her friends in the churning, foaming sea, having a great holiday.

But the sea was splashing and churning for a particular reason. They were not alone.

supersize snacks

Jean Brown was floating on her back, eyes closed and completely relaxed, when a jet of water shot up out of the ocean a few metres behind her. Janey caught sight of the little fountain, and then she saw another. And another. All around them, getting ever closer, was a circle of water jets.

Janey's heart thudded as she caught sight of something else glistening, moving fast just under the surface of the water.

'Er, Mum . . .' she called quietly. '*Everyone*, I think you should head towards me. Slowly. Don't splash.'

Jean Brown's instant response was to thrash over on to her front and kick towards Janey. 'What? What is it?'

Janey's heart sank. Only a short distance behind her mum, the water parted for a second and a slick sliver of whale-skin bobbed into view, then disappeared. The whale was closer than it had been before.

The others, responding to the warning tone in Janey's voice, had fallen silent. G-Mamma pulled on her goggles – Ultra-gogs, thought Janey – and did a neat and splashless tuck-and-dive beneath the surface. She popped up again a moment later, much closer to Janey.

'Fishy fiascos!' she squeaked. 'Killer whales!'

'No one thrash!' hissed Janey. 'Keep calm.'

The spout of water behind Mrs Brown was now so close that it actually looked to Janey as though it was coming out of the top of her mum's head. The whale could be just about to open its deadly jaws and snap her up. Hardly thinking what she was doing, and ignoring her own advice, Janey hauled herself out of the water to crouch on her ASPIC. Just as she cruised to her mother's side, the terrifying mouth reared out of the water, open, ready to strike.

'Janeeeeyy!' screeched Jean Brown.

In one movement, Janey bent down to scoop her mother up on to the front of her ASPIC and extended one leg behind her. The killer whale's teeth grazed the bare skin below her golden SPIsuit as she lifted her foot and banged hard against the whale's tongue. Her Four-Fs exploded and she and her mother shot off across the ocean, her mum straddling the board and hanging on wildly with both arms and Janey balanced on one leg like a crazed ballerina. The whale snapped its jaws together and dived under the water with a low trumpeting sound.

Janey's ASPIC collided with Alfie. He and Leaf were back-to-back on their boards, Alfie covering for Leaf as he punched questions into his PERSPIRE as quickly as his wet, slippery fingers would allow. 'Come on,' muttered Alfie. 'We're completely surrounded. Find out what we can do!'

'I am trying. This is madness. This should not be happening,' said Leaf, glancing up anxiously as a nearby waterspout showered his board with droplets of ocean.

Meanwhile Tish, G-Mamma and Mrs Halliday were all lined up on Tish's board, standing in a row and not daring to put a toe into the water as the circling waterspouts got nearer and nearer, and ominous flashes of whale-skin broke the surface.

'How many are there?' Janey pulled her mum to her feet and got her balanced on the board. 'Two? Three?'

Alfie turned to her, his face grim. 'Eleven. There are eleven of them. And six of us.'

'Supersize snacks!' yelled G-Mamma. 'That's what we'll be! Titian Ambition, don't you dare move!' Tish clearly had no intention of moving and was trying to hold the board still.

Janey put her arms around her mum's waist. For the rest of them it was terrifying, but for Jean Brown this situation was plain madness. All she knew was that a pack of killer whales had surrounded a random group of swimmers and was about to eat them up. She squeezed Janey hard and dropped a kiss on her forehead. 'I haven't protected you. That's my job, as your mother, and I've failed you.'

'No, you haven't,' said Janey fiercely. 'You're brilliant. You don't know how brilliant . . .'

'That's why everyone stayed on the beach,' said Jean quietly. 'I'm so sorry, Janey.'

Janey shook her head, gasping as water spouted up from the ocean just metres away. She glanced at the sleeping figures on the beach – and her breath caught in her throat. The eleven waterspouts were grouped in a neat circle all around them, but she wasn't looking at them. Instead her eyes fixed on one of the only figures on the beach that wasn't asleep.

Trouble.

He was lying on a towel near the beach bags, his eyes glowing hypnotically as he watched every move. Suddenly he stood up, the bristles at the back of his neck standing on end.

Right at that moment, all the jets of water died away. Janey sensed that the killer whales were waiting for something: a signal to attack. 'Trouble!' she screamed. 'Come here, Twubs! Everyone, get closer to me and Mum.'

The spy team leaped into action, paddling, ASPICing, dragging their way across the choppy water towards Janey, just as eleven sets of teeth rose out of the ocean. The whales were ready to strike the moment they were instructed to do so.

Janey looked around. And there it was – a hideous tentacle rising momentarily out of the water and slapping the surface like a conductor striking the podium with his baton. Copernicus.

She looked left. The water around them was bubbling, alive with the motion of eleven enormous bodies – twelve, now she knew the hideous Squid Man was there too.

But help was on the way.

Trouble was sleek and glorious, his golden tail streaming out behind him and his quiff flattened by the wind as he scooted across the ocean on what looked like his own tiny surfboard. Then, with an enormous yowl of satisfaction, Trouble launched himself off his board and sank his claws into one of the enormous whales. He raced up the slope of its back, jumping neatly over the spout hole and springing in a graceful somersault right off the tip of its nose . . .

. . . and straight into Janey's arms. 'Hang on, everyone!' she yelled.

Then she grabbed the little glass bell that the Spycat always wore around his neck. The bell that was actually a SPIroscope, an amazing SPI-buy that activated a powerful and dangerous vortex, protecting only those at its centre.

The SPIroscope sprang into action with

dramatic effect: the spy team was instantly lifted above the ocean in a bubble of air, while all around them chaos reigned in the awesome power of the SPIroscope. The whales were thrashing about, unable to stop themselves from being tossed around. Janey whooped with joy as whale after whale was flipped helplessly out of the water, sailing through the air and landing far, far away.

Then she saw the mutated, disfigured form of Copernicus, screeching with rage and flying through the sky, tossed up out of the ocean by Trouble's SPI-buy, tentacles twisting and thrashing helplessly. 'How . . . what . . . ?' Jean Brown stared at Janey and then back at the pandemonium outside the vortex.

Janey thought quickly. 'IMAX!' she said. 'We're in the . . . er . . . land of theme parks, remember. It's all a, um, 3D experience. Nothing to worry about at all.'

Her mother frowned and then sighed. 'Well, honestly. That was much too lifelike for my liking. And what's that – the parting of the Red Sea?'

They all followed her gaze, and Janey smothered a grin. Her SPI-buy had done its work particularly well: the SPIroscope had created a tunnel between two walls of water, reaching almost as far as the beach.

'Wow. What an effect!' Janey smiled at her mum, and moments later they were all running for the safety of the shore.

As soon as they were in the shallows Janey let go

of the SPIroscope. They waded knee-deep through the water to the beach, while behind them the twin cliffs of seawater wobbled and wavered, then collapsed in on themselves, millions of gallons crashing together in a maelstrom of sand and ocean and some rather large sea creatures.

Safely out of the waves, they collapsed in a line along the sand.

'They really should warn you when they're going to pull that kind of stunt,' said Janey's mum, staring out at the ocean.

Mrs Halliday sat up and looked around. 'There's your proof that it's just another display, Jean,' she said, pointing down the beach. 'Nobody even bothered to wake up for it.'

Janey looked at the sunbathers. It was true. Nobody had even stirred from their sleep.

'Weird,' said Alfie.

But one person was awake, and he was watching them now with solemn, dark eyes. It was the little boy, all alone, still clutching his knees to his chest and scratching his head occasionally.

Janey leaned across to G-Mamma. 'He might need brain-wiping.'

'OK, Blondelicious. I'll check him out.' She hauled herself to her feet and trotted over to the boy. 'Hello! We're going to get an ice cream. Want one?'

The boy shook his head.

89

'Candy? Doughnuts?'

Again the boy shook his head.

'Well,' said G-Mamma, perplexed – she'd offered him all her favourite things and he'd refused – 'is there anything you would like?'

And at that, the boy picked up a stick and drew in the sand. Janey now approached and looked closely at the drawing. It was a little circle on top of a big circle, with two tiny circles on either side of the bigger circle. 'Potatoes?' she asked helplessly.

The boy shook his head again sadly.

'What's your name?' said Janey.

He picked up the stick again and wrote the number twelve.

'No,' said Janey. 'Your name. Like my name is Janey.'

The little boy shrugged, picked up his stick again and pointed at the number twelve.

'Well, if you get hungry, just come and ask,' said G-Mamma, grabbing Janey's arm and walking away. 'No need to brain-wipe,' she whispered. 'He's not going to tell anyone.'

'How do you know?'

'Because I don't think he can speak,' said G-Mamma.

Janey felt so sorry for the little boy that she wanted to turn straight back to him. So that was why he had simply shaken his head and drawn pictures, blinking sadly with his dark, bitter-chocolate eyes. But the rest of their party was at the umbrella, gathering their things together, and now that the sun had sunk a little and the temperature had dropped, the other sunbathers were beginning to stir. When she looked again to see whether the boy needed her help, he had disappeared. He must have left with his family, she thought. She hoped they'd look after him.

They clambered into the huge car again to make their way back to the villas, a much more subdued party than the one that had been splashing in the sea just hours before. Janey turned to Alfie. 'How many whales did you say there were?'

Leaf spoke for him. 'Eleven! Eleven killer whales!' He sounded incredibly angry – and with good reason, thought Janey. Copernicus had just tried to wipe them all out in one go.

Janey turned and stared out of the window. Her Blonde instincts were turning over and over in her stomach, warning her that she had missed something important. Something obvious . . . It wasn't simply that Copernicus had tried to kill them all. There was something else.

She couldn't work it out now. But Jane Blonde was determined to get to the bottom of it. Soon.

r-evolution

When Jean went to bed Janey and the team gave Abe a full debrief. He peered anxiously into the camera and his face loomed up on the Spylab's plasma screen. 'Did Jean buy the "3D experience" story?' he asked.

G-Mamma sniffed. 'That woman believes anything these days. Apart from the truth. Can't we just tell—'

'No,' said Abe defiantly. 'It's not the right time. She can know all about us when she needs to. You have to remember what a shock it will be to her. Especially finding out her daughter is Jane Blonde.'

Janey could only begin to imagine what state that particular bit of information would get Jean Brown into.

She listened respectfully as the others shared their concerns with Abe. 'Nothing goes to plan,' said Leaf with a sigh.

Abe shook his head. 'So it seems. I'm sorry you all had to go through that.'

'Eleven killer whales!' said Leaf, angrily.

'Ah, there's a song in that!' G-Mamma beamed. 'Eleven killer wha-ales, ten hungry hippos, nine naughty nippers, eight angry gators, something something something . . . five . . . gold . . . rings . . .'

But Janey didn't hear much after 'ten hungry hippos'. There hadn't been ten hippos. There had been eleven. Eleven whales, and eleven hippos. And there was something else . . .

She spoke out loud. 'They weren't regular killer whales. They weren't black and white – they were *grey* and white. And they were far smaller than regular killer whales. Just like Helios was at Seaworld . . .'

'What are you getting at, Blonde?' asked Alfie.

'Yes, tell us, Janey. What's on your mind?' Her father's eyes seemed to glitter with anticipation. Janey took a deep breath.

'The whales . . . I think they *were* hippos. Something's been done to them. They've been sort of altered.'

As she spoke, Abe seemed to stagger backwards and slump into a chair, his mouth open and his face grey. 'He knows,' was all he said.

Then he shook his head and wiped a hand across his forehead, bewilderment furrowing his brow. 'He knows about Revolution. He's got ahead of me.' He fumbled around with something and then said, 'Wait for me there.'

Janey's heart jumped. Her father was coming! On the one hand that filled her with joy, but on the other it made her very nervous – if her father was coming out of hiding, he was seriously worried.

Moments later Abe materialized next to the open French windows, various cells and body parts joining up like a complex 3D jigsaw before their very eyes. As soon as he had re-formed, he locked the French windows behind him and strode across to his team. He touched Janey's arm briefly before he turned to the others.

'I have to tell you this in person. It's the most awe-inspiring, and potentially the most monstrous, discovery I've ever made.'

Janey thought about the people looking after him at Solfari Lands – Ivan Erikssen, Magenta and the Bird family. Blackbird had already betrayed him once. Abe was right to mistrust her, to get out of the way and deliver the information to them direct.

Abe stared at his feet for a moment, then sighed. 'Revolution. I sometimes wish these things never occurred to me. They seem to get the world into trouble.'

'Revolution is like . . . war, isn't it, sir?' said Alfie. He, his mother and G-Mamma moved instinctively together, closing ranks, preparing for battle.

'Yes. No. Not like you think.' Abe paced distract-edly. 'This particular revolution is a little different.'

With that he took a laser pen from his pocket, pro-jected it on to the ceiling and wrote 'R-Evolution' in large red letters. After a few moments the image faded, and the spies looked back at their leader, puzzled.

'Not really Revolution. It's R-Evolution. That's what this process is. Rapid Evolution. Using this method – which is a long way from perfected, I should add – we can take a creature in one form and speed up the way it evolves.'

'You make it grow up fast?' said Tish, saying out loud what everyone else was thinking.

Abe shrugged. 'In a manner of speaking. You make it *change* very quickly. In less than an hour, we can make a creature go through millions of years of evolution.'

There was silence while everyone worked out what this meant, then Alfie said, 'So you mean that if you had a sabretooth tiger, you could turn it into a regular tiger?'

Abe nodded gravely.

G-Mamma yelped. 'Or a mammoth into an ele-phant?'

'Yes.'

Now Janey spoke. 'And a hippo?'

Her father sighed. 'Many people don't real-ize this, but the hippo's closest relative is the

95

whale. That's what their forebears might have evolved into.'

'So Copernicus has found out about R-Evolution, stolen some hippos and changed them into killer whales?' Janey gulped. This was bad news, on so many levels. Not only did it mean that a double agent was passing information on to Copernicus; it also meant that Copernicus had yet another means of creating armies of killer creatures . . .

Abe strode around the room, thinking aloud. 'So. We have to track down Copernicus and stop him. I'm sure stealing a few hippos is just the beginning.'

Alfie spoke. 'Sir, could the process be reversed? Like could you make . . . *dinosaurs*?'

Again Abe could only nod, the tiniest movement of his head, but his eyes were filled with horror. After a moment's silence he managed to recover himself. He spoke quickly. 'Alfie, you and your mum, and Leaf, track down Copernicus for me.' He resumed his circuit of the lab. 'Tish, G-Mamma, you can come back with me. I'm going to close down the Solfari Lands Spylab. In fact, I'm stopping all R-Evolution research. It's too dangerous. I want you for extra security if anything turns nasty.'

'What about me?' asked Janey, sure that she'd have a key part to play in the next phase of the mission. But the bleak expression on her father's face worried her.

'Get your mother home,' he said. 'Make sure

you're both safe, and then wait for instructions from G-Mamma. *Please, Janey.*'

He said this even before Janey had started to argue, and though she longed to plead with him to let her stay in Florida and help track down Copernicus, she couldn't find the words. The most important thing to Abe was knowing that his family was safe. So Janey squeezed his hand, then nodded.

It was time to part. Her father set the coordinates and zoomed off by Satispy, closely followed by G-Mamma and Titian Ambition. Leaf and Alfie were already involved in a hot debate about where they should start looking for Copernicus.

'He must have a Spylab in the Everglades,' Alfie was saying.

'We should go to the ocean.' Leaf crossed his arms belligerently. 'That is where we saw him last.'

'Right,' said Alfie. 'So we go to the ocean, in the middle of the night, in the pitch black, with at least eleven killer whales . . . what am I not liking about this?'

'You are scared, I think.'

'No, not scared,' said Alfie slowly, as if he was talking to an idiot. 'Wise. Sensible. Not keen to be whale food.'

'Boys!' snapped Mrs Halliday in her best head-teacher voice. 'Let's argue about this later. First of all we need to get Janey and Jean back home, safe and sound, and that means you and I, Alfie, will have to go too to avoid suspicion. We'll zap back as quickly as possible. Go and wake your mum up, Janey. It will be dawn soon.'

Janey nodded. Dawn. A new day. She wondered how she would explain to her mum that they had to leave suddenly, but that miraculously a plane would be laid on just for them, and all their transport home would be completely organized.

'Why can't I just tell her the truth?' she grumbled as she vaulted through the French windows into her own bedroom. Her dad had made it sound like one day it would be possible. But when?

The sun was just peeking through the blinds as Janey pushed open her mum's door. 'Are you awake?' she said softly.

She pushed the door fully open, and then her knees gave way.

Her mum wasn't there. The bedside table was overturned and the bedclothes were tangled across the floor as though someone had dragged her mother from her bed, but that wasn't the worst thing.

Janey looked in horror at the black tar-like writing plastered like graffiti across the far wall, over the glass door, on her mum's dressing gown hanging on its hook – everywhere. The message said:

STAY AWAY,
BLONDE,
OR MUMMY
WILL STAY
AWAY . . .
FOREVER..

sky's the limit

Once Janey had calmed down enough to tell Mrs Halliday, Alfie and Leaf what had happened, there was more arguing over where they should head first.

'He must have taken her to the ocean,' said Leaf. 'It is the most obvious place.'

Alfie curled his lip. 'He won't have a Spylab under the ocean, duh. Way too difficult to build.'

Leaf looked at Alfie smugly. 'He might have her in a submarine, or on a boat.'

'Please, Leaf, Alfie,' Janey said desperately. 'I can't sit here arguing.' Janey was so tired of keeping secrets from her mum that right now she had sworn to herself she would tell her everything if – no, *when* – she found her.

'Blonde is right,' said Mrs Halliday, jumping to her feet. 'Alfie, since you're so sure he must be in the Everglades, you go there. Janey, you go with him. Leaf, you and I will go and check out the ocean site we were at earlier.'

The boys knew better than to argue with such authority, and within minutes they had Satispied to their respective destinations. Janey's heart bumped around in the bottom of her chest. It didn't matter whether her mum was trapped in the Everglades or under the ocean: in either place she would be frightened and lonely, and worried for Janey. She had to be found.

Once they had rematerialized by the river, Alfie's eyes lit up. 'Allow me,' he said, leaping on to the swamp buggy and revving the engine loudly.

'Just make it quick,' was all Janey said as she braced herself for the ride.

And quick it was. Janey was nearly flung off into alligator-infested waters as Alfie careered across the Everglades, tracking his progress in his Ultra-gogs and shouting out landmarks to assure Janey he knew where he was going. 'Duck under these branches. That's right. Yep, tree shaped like an ice-cream cone – nearly there. Last bend, hold on.'

Suddenly they were at the spot at which Janey had found the hippos. She leaped on to the slippery bank, little caring whether any alligators had spotted her. Then she signalled to Alfie, shoved a SPIder in her mouth and plunged into the water.

The Ultra-gogs adjusted immediately, giving

her relatively clear vision through the gloom of the water. There were a couple of alligators nearby, but they didn't seem at all interested in her. Janey flicked out the titanium blade from the finger of her Girl-gauntlet, just in case, and went deeper. There was no sign of a Spylab, and Janey's spy instincts told her that her mum wasn't anywhere near.

She touched a foot to the riverbed to turn around and head back to Alfie, and just then noticed something twinkling in the mud as a shaft of sunlight penetrated the water. Something that looked out of place on the sludgy riverbed. Janey dug it out with her blade and swam up to the surface.

Wiping it clean with her Gauntlet, Janey inspected her find. It was a mirror: a tiny round mirror on the end of a stick, rather like a lollipop. She waded quickly over to the swamp buggy and clambered aboard.

'Alfie, I found . . . Alfie!'

Her Spylet friend was fast asleep, slumped across the rudder like a puppet whose strings had been cut. So much for looking out for her. When Janey shook him he lifted his head and peered at her with one eye. ''S 'ot.'

'What?'

'It's hot,' he said more clearly, stretching his arms. 'Find anything?'

Janey showed him the little mirror. 'Only this. Could be a clue though.'

'It looks like one of those things a dentist would use.' Alfie turned the mirror this way and that, looking for marks of some kind. 'Argh!' he cried.

A shaft of sunlight had bounced off the mirror straight into Alfie's eyes. He twitched it out of the way, and Janey watched, fascinated, as the beam of light headed straight back up the river behind them. If anyone had been at the picnic site, they would have seen the light instantly.

'It's to signal with,' said Janey excitedly. Angling the mirror carefully, she managed to direct the sunlight up against a tree, then straight into the eye of an overcurious alligator who very quickly sank out of sight.

Whipping off her PERSPIRE, she tapped in 'signal mirror' and waited for the information to pop up inside the cap. 'Here we are. Safety mirrors for outdoor pursuits. Well, this is certainly outdoors. That must be it.'

'Or,' said Alfie, peeking over her shoulder, 'maybe it's something to do with that.'

He pointed to the article at the bottom of the page. *An astronaut's survival kit,* it said, *consists of a parachute, inflatable boat, two days' drinking water, signal mirror . . .*

Janey's head spun. Alfie was right. 'That's it,' she said solemnly. 'Copernicus had that rocket, didn't he?' He'd been trying to escape Antarctica in it last time they had been pitted against each other. 'But where would he be keeping a rocket? Not under the ocean . . .'

Then suddenly it came to her, and dread filled Janey's stomach. In her mind's eye she travelled back to the day she had been flicking through her mum's brochures for Florida tourist attractions. And at once it all made perfect, horrible sense.

The Everglades, the ocean, the hippos, the killer whales – they weren't as important as what was built on a small island just off the Florida coast . . .

'I know where he is,' she said to Alfie. 'I know where his lab is and where he's got Mum.'

Alfie spun the swamp buggy around without a second's hesitation, and in seconds they were back at the picnic site, ready to Satispy.

'Where are we headed?' Alfie waited to tap in the coordinates for their safe landing.

Janey consulted her Ultra-gogs once more. It had to be right. 'The Space Center,' she said. 'Cape Canaveral.'

'Oh my life,' groaned Alfie as he threw her the remote and disintegrated into a steady stream of cells, flowing skywards.

Copernicus wanted to reach the stars, thought Janey. But she was going to stop him.

cape capers

To Janey's horror, she materialized directly in front of a large crowd of awestruck schoolchildren. 'Alfie,' she hissed, frantically looking around.

'And . . . er . . . don't miss the show later,' she heard him say. 'Holograph spectacular, 1 p.m.'

Alfie was standing just behind her. Janey took the hint and waved at the children, half of whom already looked bored – or just plain tired – and were wandering off to the next exhibit.

Alfie picked up a visitor's guide that one of the children had dropped. The child was now propped in a nearby seat, enjoying a morning nap.

'What is wrong with everyone?' said Janey, staring at the child and then at the map. 'So we're in the Visitor Complex of the Space Center. Where would The Big C be hiding?'

Alfie had retreated into a bush and was busy SPIVing his mum, so Janey studied the leaflet.

There was a garden to the left of them, with a collection of grounded rockets, and behind that a curious dome that looked like a possible Spylab location. To the right there was a black spherical structure that appeared to be floating on its own little lake. Copernicus had a passion for black, so Janey decided to check this out first.

Mrs Halliday and Leaf Satispied discreetly behind some trees at the back of the Rocket Garden and ran over, Alfie in tow. 'Where would he have put your mother, Janey?' said Mrs Halliday, laying a hand on Janey's shoulder.

Janey felt a rush of warmth for the matter-of-fact SPI:KE. No matter how dangerous the plans of the mad Copernicus might be, Agent Halo knew that nothing was more important to Janey than finding her mum. 'I was wondering about this black ball thing.'

'I am thinking he would like the dome,' said Leaf, pointing to the left.

'Well, let's split up.' Janey pointed over to the black sphere. 'We'll go that way,' she said, nodding to Alfie, 'and Halo and Leaf can check out the dome.'

'Why don't you come with me?' asked Leaf, but Janey and Alfie were already picking their way through the crowds.

Janey reached the sphere several paces before Alfie. She turned and waited for him to catch up, and he staggered to her side. 'Don't know what's the matter with me,' he said, panting. 'This weather's just too much.'

'It doesn't matter,' said Janey. 'This can't be it anyway.'

They both looked at the black sphere. There were small children hanging off the orb, trying to push it around its little lake. Their teacher had given up and barely responded when one of the children prodded him in the thigh.

'It's too busy,' said Janey. 'He wouldn't risk being this open, particularly in his current freaky state.'

Suddenly her SPIV bounced against her chest, and she peered at it to see Leaf's thin, upside-down face. 'Blonde,' he whispered, 'we've found a Spylab entry tube. This must be it.'

There was a bit of confusion on the tiny screen and then Mrs Halliday's face appeared. 'I'm not so sure, Leaf. It just looks like a kids' slide to me.'

'But I think Blonde should come and check it out . . .'

'No,' said Janey quietly. Remembering what form Copernicus was in, she took another look at the map. 'I've worked it out, I think. Come over to Space Shuttle Plaza.'

She showed Alfie the map as she started to jog over to the Plaza. 'Look, there's a space shuttle there that you can actually go on, and a lake next to it.'

Alfie nodded. 'Could be it. Look, you . . . ow,

I've got a stitch . . . you run on ahead. I'll catch up with you.'

'Come *on*, Alfie,' she said, linking her arm through his so she could half drag him along as she ran. It wasn't too difficult to make progress, despite the crowds and the extra weight of Alfie. Most visitors seemed to be flaking out on the grassy verges, taking forty winks or walking along sluggishly. In a matter of minutes they were at Space Shuttle Plaza. 'Look, Alfie,' she said, staring in awe at the shuttle. A real rocket, and anyone could go inside.

Alfie's head lolled back. 'Awesome,' he yawned.

'This is it; I can just feel it. And . . . yes!' Janey let Alfie slide to the ground and ran around the shuttle. There, beside the water, was a tar-like slick – revolting squid ink, secreted by Copernicus as he hauled himself out of the water and into his lab.

She moved closer to the pool. It made sense for the lab to be closer to the lake, as most people would be more interested in the shuttle itself. Although that wasn't the case today, thought Janey. Few people seemed to have the strength to climb the steps to the shuttle door. In fact there was hardly anyone around apart from Alfie, who was leaning against a bin with his head in his hands. Leaf and Mrs Halliday were coming up behind him, both moving slowly, Leaf propping up Agent Halo in the same way Janey had had to support Alfie.

And then she saw it, winking next to the pool. A tiny disc. Excited, Janey pressed it, but nothing happened. She pressed again, waving to the others to join her, but still nothing happened.

'Mi-mirror,' panted Alfie, his hands on his knees and his hair dark with sweat.

'Of course!' Janey fished out the signal mirror from the Everglades and held it at different angles until a shaft of light shot from the signal mirror and connected with the silver disc on the ground. Like ripples on a pond, the light flooded outwards, and Janey found herself staring straight down a wide tube leading directly, she was sure, into one of Copernicus's Spylabs.

'I'll go first,' she said, then stopped short.

It appeared she wasn't just going to go first. She was going alone. Mrs Halliday had joined Alfie next to the bin and was fast asleep. She was surprised to see that Leaf had curled up on the grass and was also close to sleep.

Janey looked around. Every single person was asleep – all the Space Center staff, all the tourists and now all the SPIs. All apart from, Janey realized, a woman in a yellow sundress, who was chucking water from a bottle over her boyfriend, trying to stir him into action.

There was no waking Alfie or Mrs Halliday, but Leaf came to when Janey poked at him with her foot. 'Come on. I've got to rescue my mum. And then we'll see what's wrong with everyone.'

'Yes, yes,' he said, brushing grass off his SPIsuit, so that Janey just caught a glimpse of gold beneath the green of his cuff. 'I am coming now, Blonde.'

One after the other they jumped down the entry tube into the lab. It looked exactly as Janey had expected: shimmering, black, lit only by a few holes in the ceiling. The only things that weren't black were their two SPIsuits, and a glint of white in a chair. A blouse. A once-neat but now dishevelled white blouse.

'Mum!'

Janey ran over in an instant. Her mum was bound to the chair with some kind of cable, and her head jerked forward at the sound of Janey's voice. 'Darling! Oh, you shouldn't have come here.'

'I've come to rescue you.' Janey flicked out her titanium blade and sawed through the cable.

'But the Squid Man . . .' whispered her mother. 'He'll be back any minute, and he's been talking about you, saying all these ridiculous things about you being a . . . a *Spylet*? Whatever that is. Apparently you keep spoiling his plans and now he's going to spoil *your* plans. Don't let him find you here!'

'I won't, Mum. Can you stand up?' She helped her mother to her feet.

Jean Brown swayed alarmingly. 'I'm so sleepy. His light . . . it makes me so sleepy. And that noise . . .'

'What noise?'

Janey leaned into the silence and suddenly heard a very strange sound, a kind of hysterical chattering. She draped her mum's arm over her shoulder. 'Come on. I'll get you out of here. There's all sorts of strange stuff I need to tell you, but I promise I'll explain everything to you just as soon as I can.'

'OK,' said Mrs Brown meekly. The strain of her kidnapping seemed to have taken all the fight out of her. Or maybe it was the heat, which seemed to have extracted the fizz from just about everybody.

Janey looked around for a Satispy remote control. It would be the quickest and easiest way to get her mum to safety.

Leaf had already spotted one over on a shelf at the far side of the Spylab. 'Great,' said Janey. 'I'll send my mum first, maybe to Dad at Solfari Lands. Then, if you help me get the Halos downstairs, I'll send them, and then you, and I'll go last.'

But Leaf wasn't responding. Instead he was staring over Janey's shoulder, an anxious expression on his face, and Janey could just *feel* what – who – must be standing behind her.

The tall figure of Copernicus loomed between her and the remote control. By his side was someone Janey had almost forgotten about – the little boy from the beach, who had been watching them so seriously and had written his name in the sand: Twelve.

'Right,' said Janey. 'No wonder he doesn't

have a name if he's just one of your Spylets. He's a bit young, though, isn't he?'

Copernicus exhaled – a long, slow expulsion of air that seemed to fill the lab with evil – and the strange chattering, laughing sound from beyond the lab grew louder. 'Blonde, Blonde, Blonde . . . you have managed to cause me enough trouble despite your tender years. How young is too young?' He laughed bitterly. 'Actually he's even younger than you think.'

Janey flicked her eyes towards Leaf. If they could get hold of the remote somehow, the Satispy could at least zap her mother out of here. But Leaf appeared to be transfixed, entranced by Copernicus. She was on her own. 'Well, if you'll just excuse me,' she said, trying for an almighty bluff, 'I've just got to get my mum home. By the way, your son's up there.' And she nodded at the tube, hoping to distract her enemy.

But Copernicus rounded on her like a viper. 'Your mother goes nowhere. At least, not with you. She can come with me when I take off very, very shortly. Didn't I tell you? Stay away. Or Mummy stays away . . .'

'Forever,' finished Leaf. He looked helplessly at Janey.

So that was it. They were trapped. Alfie and Mrs Halliday had been sedated or something. Leaf had been frozen into inactivity by the close presence of evil incarnate. Janey herself was hampered by her mother's weight as Jean Brown tried, and failed, to regain the use of her legs. The only person who seemed alert was the little boy – Twelve – whose head tilted longingly in the direction of the jabbering laughter.

And Janey suddenly realized something. Twelve was distracted. Maybe he wasn't a tiny Spylet at all – he was far too interested in what was going on beyond the laboratory walls. Just like a normal little boy would be.

Which meant that, if her instincts were right, he wouldn't try to stop her if she made a lunge for the remote control.

And with a quiet, 'Sorry, Mum,' in her mother's ear, she thrust Jean across the lab towards Copernicus. To Janey's immense relief, she discovered she had made the right assumption about Copernicus. He was simply a Retro-spectre – a holographic image made up from memories of what he used to be like before Jane Blonde had given him tentacles.

Jean Brown fell to the floor, sliding straight through the wispy body of Copernicus. In seconds Janey flew across, grabbed the remote from the shelf and Satispied her bewildered mother into space, hopefully back to the safety of Solfari Lands.

Then she pocketed the control, grabbed Leaf by the arm and made a break for the outside. For sunshine. For safety.

13 countdown

Janey and Leaf bounced out of the entry tube and landed just in front of Alfie and Mrs Halliday. They had barely moved and were slumped against each other, ignoring the flies that were crawling across their faces.

'Alfie! Halo. Al Halo.' Janey hissed at them, but they merely blinked. 'Oh, this is hopeless!'

Leaf, at least, seemed to have pulled himself together. 'So what now?'

'Copernicus is stealing a rocket. This place isn't just for tourists – rockets really do take off from here, and he's going to steal one. Let's get over to the Control Center. I think he's planning to launch soon.'

A quick glance at the information leaflet informed her that the Launch Control Center was over to their right. In normal circumstances it would have required a long walk. But these were not normal circumstances. 'Everyone's so dozy they won't notice us Fleet-footing,' said Janey decisively. 'Come on.'

Leaf hesitated for only a second, irritation flashing briefly across his face. Like Alfie, thought Janey. He doesn't like being upstaged by a girl. 'OK. I come too,' said the green-suited Spylet, and he sprinted off across the grass in the direction of the Launch Center.

Only the woman in the yellow dress, who had given up trying to revive her boyfriend and was now eating her way through their picnic bag, had the energy to say, 'What the . . . ?' as they sped by, and moments later they were approaching the Launch Center. The pale concrete building glowed ominously in the brilliant sunshine.

Leaf jolted to a halt at Janey's side.

'Copernicus has probably gone in from underneath,' she said. 'We'll have to be careful.'

Splitting up, they ran around the exterior of the building, but found no evidence and met up again in front of the main door. More out of curiosity than anything else, Janey gave it a gentle shove. Despite the obvious entry-card system, the door swung open.

They exchanged glances and stepped through. Directly ahead was a large desk that should have been bustling with security guards. Instead there was one weary woman with her chin on the desk.

'This is the Launch Control Center, isn't it?' Janey looked around uncertainly, and then peeked over the desk. Two security guards were stretched out on the floor next to the woman's chair, snoring roundly.

'Last time I looked,' said the woman with a yawn. 'But in this heat, who the heck cares?'

'But . . .'

Leaf grabbed Janey's arm. 'Thank you. Then we will just . . .' and he pointed down the corridor.

'Sure.' The woman nuzzled her head down on to her arms. 'Wake me up on your way back.'

Janey frowned at her, then ran quickly after Leaf. Every door swung open at their touch, and every security person, scientist and engineer they passed was either sound asleep or so relaxed that they simply waved to them, rubbing their foreheads and trying to clamp their jaws around yet another yawn.

'This is really weird,' said Janey. Then she gasped.

They had reached a corridor with a huge bank of windows on either side. On the left she could see a large rocket in the distance. On the right the two Spylets looked down on a room peopled by dozing engineers and labelled with distinctive signs: MAIN PROPULSION SYSTEMS; LIQUID OXYGEN; REACTION CONTROL SYSTEM.

'The Launch Control Center,' said Leaf with a glint in his eye.

It was hugely impressive, and Janey wished that Alfie could see it too – the ultimate in boys' toys. But there was no time to lose, because drifting around the centre of the room, holographic eyes fixed on a screen showing the same huge rocket they could see through the windows, was a sinister Retro-spectre of Copernicus as he had once been.

'We have to be quick! He's brain-wiped everyone or something. They're under his control.'

Janey chewed quickly on a tiny piece of SPInamite, stuck it on to one of the window frames and covered her head and Leaf's. There was a small explosion and a rain of glass that caused some of the engineers below to sluggishly lift their heads from the desks and computer keyboards. Now Janey was standing next to a neat hole in the window. As fast as she could, she unwound her SuSPInder and abseiled down into the Launch Control Center. Leaf quickly followed.

Janey ran across to the nearest engineer and shook him by his shoulder. 'That man's stealing a rocket.'

The man blinked blearily at her. 'He can have it.'

'Have it? It's a rocket!'

Janey couldn't believe what she was hearing. She looked around. All the engineers looked equally relaxed about the fact that a strange man was making off with one of their most prized possessions. 'It's a matter of national security,' she yelled. 'International. Global even!'

'Well . . . whatever,' said the man with a

shrug, and he propped his forehead against his computer monitor and drifted off to sleep.

The Retro-spectre of Copernicus had barely taken his eyes off the screen. A countdown, in important-looking red numbers, was flashing in the top right-hand corner.

19.30.

'You're completely wasting your time,' said the Retro-spectre, not even bothering to look at Janey. 'But then you're good at that, aren't you, Blonde? Wasting time. Especially . . . mine!'

Janey didn't care. He could sound as threatening as he liked. He was just a hologram: a ghost really, and ghosts couldn't hurt her. She had nineteen and a half minutes and she had to make every second count. Running straight through the image of Copernicus, Janey called out to Leaf, 'Flick switches. Press alarm buttons. Do something – anything – that stops that rocket taking off.'

18.40.

But Leaf seemed incapable of doing anything at all when Copernicus was around, even in Retro-spectre form, so Janey had to do everything herself. She sped along the banks of computers, tipping water into keyboards and doing whatever she could to make the launch falter.

17.20.

'It's all pre-programmed,' said the Retro-spectre.

'And, of course, I'm not really here. Do you honestly think I would be stupid enough to leave something like this to chance?'

16.50

'Something like what?' said Janey helplessly.

The Retro-spectre turned to her with a vile sneer. 'My planet. My chance to rule the universe. At long last.'

15.55.

So it was that again. 'You're mad. You can't rule the universe on your own. And you're not taking Alfie this time,' she said.

15.10.

'No, I won't be taking Alfie. He will be . . . disposed of.' Copernicus eyed her with something approaching sadness. 'But I will not be alone.'

Janey's heart sank. 'Where's Alfie? How can you kill your own son?'

14.40

'It is regretful,' said Copernicus with a sigh. 'But he has shown where his loyalties lie. I have new off-spring now who will stand by me.'

Janey followed his eyes to the rocket. Cages were being loaded on to it. Cages she had seen before. Filled with . . . monkeys.

'They're apes,' she said. 'Not people.'

13.20.

Copernicus simply smiled, and then laughed, the horrible keening sound whistling through the

Control Center. 'They are not people. But I think you met my new son.'

And he turned around and pointed to a little boy, all fitted out in a spacesuit, climbing aboard the rocket.

'Twelve,' said Janey softly.

'Oh, at least. And many more.' Copernicus laughed again. 'I'll have everyone I need with me. And you, Blonde, will be long gone.'

11.40.

Janey had no idea what he meant, but at that moment two doors opened opposite each other, and a pair of gorillas pounded along the pathways between the computers towards her.

'Back to the Spylab,' snapped Copernicus as two huge hairy hands grasped her arms, 'and then suit up and get on the launch pad before the lab explosion. I'll be taking the tube. You've only got . . .'

10.01

'. . . ten minutes,' whispered Janey, slithering help-lessly along the tiled floor as the gorillas thrust her through a door and into a narrow, barely lit corridor.

Ten minutes until the rocket took off. Ten minutes until Coprnicus left the Earth behind. Ten minutes until he blew up the Spylab and everything in it.

When Janey was flung into the Spylab beneath Space Shuttle Plaza, her heart sank. Alfie and his mother were sitting on the same chair Jean Brown had been strapped to, but were tied up to a sink. Both were still snoring and dribbling.

There was an outraged snarl from the other side of the room, and Janey spun round, expecting to see the gorillas again but finding instead a furious G-Mamma, cocooned as if by a spider in a length of cable so that only her nostrils, eyes and hair poked out. Beside her lay Tish, mummified in exactly the same way.

Janey ran across and sliced through their bonds with her titanium blade. 'What are you doing here?'

'Me? What are you doing here, Blonde Bomb-shell?' G-Mamma shimmied her way out of the cable. 'This place is about to blow. I thought *you'd* escape at least.'

'We tried to get in touch with everyone, but nobody was answering,' explained Tish, rubbing her arms vigorously. 'So Abe sent us back. We ran straight into some . . . well, apes . . . and they brought us in here.'

'This is bad.' Janey knew just how bad. 'We've got about seven minutes to get out of here.'

The three of them skidded around the room, trying to locate an escape route. Janey tried SPInamiting the sealed entry tube but could only blow a hole the size of a fist. Copernicus must have had it specially reinforced. Janey even sent a flurry of desperate emails, realizing, grimly, that the screensaver showed the soon-to-be-stolen rocket, the countdown (now at 3.20) and the numbers 28.6178N and 80.6125W.

There was no reply.

2.40.

Janey ran to the Hallidays. 'Please wake up! We need to get out of here.'

'They've been sedated,' said Tish, not very help-fully. 'Sound asleep.'

1.50.

'Well, I think it's time for a final rap.' G-Mamma flexed her hands in front of her. 'Ahem . . .

'We're on our way to that Spyland above
But luckily with the people we love
And when we get there we'll find with glee
Who finally gets rid of the evil C.'

'Let's hear it for the Sol Spies! Whooooooo!'

1.25.

Janey thought of something . . . and almost smiled. 'G-Mamma, say that again.'

1.10.

With a beam and the glimmer of a tear in her eye, G-Mamma sang out: 'Finally my gift is appreciated! When it's too late. Ah well . . .'

'We're on our way to that Spyland above.
But—'

122

0.55

'That's it,' said Janey. 'Roll the Halos under the entry tube and join them.'

0.45

'No good, Blonde,' said Tish. 'If you're trying to Satispy, the remote's missing.'

0.30.

'Oh no, it's not,' said Janey, and she pulled it out from the sleeve of her golden SPIsuit, where she had stowed it earlier.

0.20.

She only hoped that the coordinates she was keying in would take her where she thought they would.

10.

'. . . 78N and 80.6125W.'

9.

8.

7.

6.

5.

4.

3.

'Hang on, everyone!'

2.

And as the blinking numbers turned to 1, and the Spylab juddered with a teeth-chattering explosion, Janey watched the others disintegrate into streams of cells and knew that the same thing was happening to herself as they Satispied out through the atmosphere, through a hole the size of a fist, and chased the rocket that was now hurtling through the skies almost as fast as they were.

Poor Leaf, Janey thought as she disintegrated. She just hoped he was safe, wherever he was.

space race

As Janey had desperately hoped, they materialized together again inside the rocket that Copernicus had stolen and now launched.

When Janey's eyeballs had popped themselves back into their sockets she found that she was the last to arrive. They were in some sort of baggage hold, except that the baggage wasn't being held. And it was rather unusual baggage.

Her feet, newly reattached, left the floor, and Janey found herself floating upside down towards the ceiling. Or was it the floor? It was all very hard to tell. G-Mamma, giving her a gleeful thumbs-up, was whipping around in somersaults and bouncing off the cylindrical walls, looking positively graceful and ballerina-like. Tish reached out to try to grab her every now and again but found it impossible to time her movements correctly, and so she too was spinning around the hold in a flurry of red. Alfie, meanwhile, having received a rather rude awakening, was holding on to his mother's shirt.

There were other bodies floating around the hold too. Wearing an array of bewildered, excited and downright cross expressions, a dozen or more members of the ape family pirouetted around them, looking completely mystified.

'The poor things!' Janey dropped her voice to a whisper; she didn't want Copernicus to hear them. 'What is he doing with them?'

Alfie spun round to face her, and kept spinning. He slowed himself by grabbing hold of G-Mamma's foot and glared, upside down, at Janey. 'Never mind what he's doing to *them*! What are *you* doing to *us*? Where are we?'

'Um. On the rocket.' Janey could understand Alfie's confusion. 'You were all tied up in the Spylab, and I got thrown in too, and it was just about to explode, so I used the Space Center coordinates to follow Copernicus when he launched.'

Alfie looked thunderous for a moment and then suddenly his shoulders dropped. 'Fair enough,' he said gruffly.

Janey took this to mean, 'Well done – good choice – all you could do in the circumstances,' and turned her attention to the apes that were floating around the hold. 'Let's try and get them under control. Make them hold hands or something,' she said.

G-Mamma led the way, grabbing hold of a passing chimpanzee. 'Titian, get its other hand. Paw. Thing with fingers.'

As soon as Tish got hold of the other hand, the chimp seemed to relax. It let out a wild chattering that the other chimps, at least, seemed to understand, and another one latched itself on to Tish's free hand and reached for a nearby gorilla. Janey glided around the rocket, orchestrating the hand-holding, and even persuaded Alfie to take his mother's hand in his right one and hold a tiny spider monkey in his left. Before too long the SPIs, Spylets and apes lined the cylindrical hold like a chain of paper dolls, and the chattering subsided to the occasional whimper.

Eventually Janey dared to glance out of the porthole. The Earth blinked below them, a sequin of blue and white on the spangled counterpane of the sky. Just then the porthole filled up. They were shooting past something . . . something grey but luminous, with a pitted surface . . .

'Crikey!' squeaked Alfie. 'You know what that is?'

G-Mamma leaned over to the porthole. 'No. Way. Is that . . . ? Do you think it's made of cheese?'

At that moment Mrs Halliday came to. 'Trust you, Rosie. We appear to be hurtling past the moon and you're thinking about food. I say the more important issue is: *where on earth are we going?*'

'We're not going anywhere on Earth,' said Janey. 'He must have finally done it.'

'Done what?' asked Tish.

It was hard to believe. Impossible even. But Copernicus had managed the impossible before, and Janey had long ago realized that he would stop at nothing to meet his bizarre and mind-shattering aims. 'He's always been obsessed with the idea that he should rule the world, the universe even. I overheard him talking in Antarctica. He was trying to steal some of the Earth's core so that he could Supersize it with his weird machine – to create gravity.'

'Why would he do that?' said Alfie.

Janey heaved a great sigh. 'So he could build his own planet.'

The others stared at her, bobbing up and down. Even the apes seemed to be gazing at her in disbelief. Janey couldn't blame them. It did sound completely mad, but before she had time to explain herself further the porthole once again filled with light, and they all turned to look.

'That's the sun,' gasped Tish. 'It's so *golden*.'

Alfie peered out of the glazed panel. 'It can't be the sun – we'd melt.'

'And we wouldn't be able to look directly at the sun, surely? You can't even do that from the Earth,' said Mrs Halliday.

'Frying eyes, you're right!' whooped G-Mamma.

'It's too small to be the sun. So what is it? And . . . is that me or are we slowing down? Whoa!'

G-Mamma's last shriek was muffled by her skirt falling over her face as the rocket slowly rotated, and the ring of people and primates found itself upside down and bouncing around, out of control. Suddenly the chain collapsed in a heap at the bottom of the hold.

'Mum, get your foot out of my nose,' grunted Alfie.

'I can't! I can't move at all.'

G-Mamma's faint voice buffeted through from the bottom of the pile. 'You should worry. I've got a manky old monkey bottom on my head . . .'

'Shh!' urged Janey. 'Hide! There's someone coming.'

Footsteps were rattling directly overhead. They had clearly landed, somewhere in space, on the surface of the strange, golden planet. Janey listened hard as she wriggled herself down between an orang-utan and a couple of chimps, checking that the other spies were also ducking out of sight. The footsteps above were quick, light – not the step-swish-drag of an enormous squid-like creature. At least it wasn't Copernicus.

As a hatch over their heads slid open, Janey hissed to her Ultra-gogs. 'Periscope,' she said, trying to avoid getting a mouthful of monkey fur.

Success! Instantly, the left lens slid across

129

to cover the right, then a slender crooked tube, like the handle of an umbrella, rose up between the bodies in the hold. Janey had a clear view. She held her breath . . .

The figure that appeared above them, however, was not in the least bit frightening. Even though she knew that the person in the spacesuit peering down into the hold was the son and loyal supporter of her arch-enemy, Janey couldn't help thinking that Twelve looked rather sad behind his helmet.

At once the chimpanzees started to chatter and surge. Janey panicked. What if they all moved? The spies would be seen!

But to her relief Twelve shook his head, once, twice, very firmly at a gibbering chimpanzee who was now jumping up and down ecstatically on what Janey was sure was Alfie's head. He gave the chimp a little wave in one smooth circular movement, put his finger to roughly where his mouth would be beneath the helmet, then held up his hands.

'Zoom!' breathed Janey to her Ultra-gogs, and they focused in.

What was he doing? First he held up his left hand and linked his right pinky around his left one. Then he used his right index finger to point at his fourth finger on his left hand. And again. Next, holding out his left palm, he tapped two fingers of his right hand against it. Then he nodded carefully to the chimp and waggled his hand. 'He's saying goodbye,' whispered Janey as he slid the hatch door shut.

'Has it gone?' whispered G-Mamma hysterically. 'Because I'm about to suffocate!'

Janey sat up cautiously and G-Mamma wiggled out between two orang-utans, so hot, red and cross that she looked like one of their relatives.

Now Mrs Halliday and the Spylets poked up out of the pile of hairy bodies and the apes resumed their restless chattering.

'It was that little boy from the beach,' Janey explained quickly. 'Copernicus says he's his son. His new, *loyal* son.'

'Oh dear,' said Alfie in a flat voice. 'He doesn't need me any more. Tragedy. Boo hoo.'

He stopped abruptly as a fresh barrage of noise filtered down from above. There was a sound like lift doors opening, then a clattering against the side of the rocket, and the SPI team looked swiftly out of the porthole.

There were five figures making their way down a ladder, weighted down by their special space boots. The two larger figures were pushing a third, adult-sized person along in front of them. Janey recognized them instantly from the way they hunched over – it was the two gorillas from the Launch Control Center. The boy called Twelve was out in front, treading in laborious steps across to some location that Janey couldn't see. Behind him came a taller figure, slender, more agile. But it was only when the gorillas pushed so hard that the adult figure stumbled and fell, and the slender figure spun round to see what was going on, that Janey was able to work out who they were.

One was someone that Janey had been wondering about. Leaf, his pale features flattened by the screen of his space helmet, was shouting something at the adult trying to get up off the ground.

Janey gasped. On a distant planet, way out in who-knew-where, far, far from home was the last person she expected – or wanted – to see.

'Mum,' she whispered, 'what are you doing here?'

15 japes with apes

'Wasn't that—' Alfie started.

'Yes,' said Janey quietly. 'I've got to follow them.'

She looked around for some means of escape. Pointing her Girl-gauntleted hand at the inner wall of the rocket, she prepared to laser, cut, blast her way out of there – anything to get to her mum as quickly as possible.

'Blondette!' shrieked G-Mamma. 'What are you doing? You cut a hole in this thing and we could all die instantly.'

'Oh.' Janey sat back on her heels, disappointed. 'That's true. We don't even know if it's air out there.'

'Judging by the way Copper Knickers's new son was wearing a spacesuit, I'm thinking no,' said Tish.

The spacesuit! That gave Janey an idea. 'I need to get up to the hatch,' she said, pointing above their heads to where Twelve had appeared.

'Your Four-Fs won't get you that far,' Alfie

pointed out. 'And you don't have your ASPIC with you.'

'No,' said Janey, 'but we do have some super-strong people launchers.' She looked at a pair of small gorillas and grinned back at Alfie.

'It's a monkey puzzle.' G-Mamma gauged the distance to the hatch. 'How many gorillas does it take to throw a Spylet ten metres?'

'Answer: all of them,' said Janey.

The SPIs and Spylets formed the first ring, the base of a tower. On their shoulders the orang-utans balanced obligingly. It appeared that nothing was too strange a request for them. Next came the chimpanzees, with the smaller monkeys looped around their arms, strengthening the joints, and finally, after a bit of coaxing and some very strange mimes, Janey persuaded the two young gorillas to scamper up the swaying human-and-ape scaffolding and position themselves at the top.

She'd seen it in Cirque du Soleil. And if ordinary people could do it, surely a Spylet with ace gadgetry could manage it. With a deep breath, Janey hauled herself up the tottering tower, slipping slightly when one of the chimpanzees suddenly moved a long arm, and trying to ignore G-Mamma huffing, 'Slowly, slowly catchy monkey,' every few seconds. Finally she reached the top. Hoping beyond all hope that the gorillas understood and wouldn't decide to thump her, she gently placed their hands together and climbed on to the little launch pad they'd created.

The hatch was now six metres above her head. Unwinding her SuSPInder from her waist, she looped it over her arm like a lasso, shouted, 'Ready! On three,' then showed one, then two, then three fingers to the gorillas. And as her three fingers fell the gorillas gibbered manically and tossed her into the air. Like a cork from a champagne bottle she shot upwards, unravelling her SuSPInder and throwing it towards the hatch. The line went taut. The tiny grappling hook had lodged itself in the rim of the hatch; now she just had to haul herself up.

'Erm, problem,' she shouted down to the others. 'There's no handle on this side.'

There was a general muttering from below, then Alfie shouted something.

'*Forget it?* No way, Al!'

'No,' he hollered back. '*Four-F* it!'

Ah. Four-F. Good idea. Janey swung upside down as the apes below grunted their approval, then she clamped her feet on to the underside of the metal hatch. She tried not to think about how she was hanging like a bat, ten metres up in the air. With superhuman effort she straightened herself out as much as possible, hanging grimly on to the SuSPInder cord, and pushed up and sideways at the same time.

It had been a *great* idea. The hatch opened

just a crack, then a little more as Janey slid her feet to the side. When it was just about wide enough, she popped her feet through the gap so that she was hanging from her knees, then pulled the rest of her body up. Rather clumsily she managed to wriggle through the gap until she found herself upright in a small cube of a room. Along one wall was a rail loaded with spacesuits, and to the other side was a small ladder leading to a similar hatch above her head.

Janey found a remote control attached to the wall. She yanked it free and dropped it through the hatch. 'It's an airlock,' she shouted down to her friends. 'I'll have to close this door before I can open the next one. But there's the remote so you can open it from that side.' Then, 'Come on, Blonde,' she told herself sternly. 'Before there's a traffic jam.' Already a line of apes was wriggling up the SuSPInder cord. In no time at all they'd be catching up with her.

She quickly donned one of the spacesuits and sped up the ladder, pressing the green button that opened the hatch. 'Wow,' she whistled when she was inside the next segment of the rocket. This was no empty holding area. All around her were flashing lights, tubes and ducts, banks of buttons and dials, tanks, turbos . . . Jane Blonde was deep within the operation room of the rocket. This section had seats too, on which the astronauts would be held down in a complex web of straps and buckles. Five seats, counted Janey. A chair for everyone who'd got off. So where had Copernicus been sitting?

There was no time to consider that. He had her mum at his mercy somewhere on this golden planet. She stepped outside and she could hardly believe it: she was actually walking in space. 'Wow,' she said again.

The feeling was unlike anything she had ever known. Excitement, fear, exhilaration – all piled up on top of each other with a headiness that could easily make a person go a little mad. She wanted to throw herself off the ladder . . . float out into the galaxy . . . feel what it was like to be such a minuscule, atom-sized, unimportant part of this amazing, staggering creation . . .

Just in time, she remembered that someone *had* actually gone mad, *had* tried to be part of the creation process. And more to the point – they were holding her mum hostage. Janey forced herself off the ladder on to the surface of the planet. It felt firm underfoot – just like the Earth really, though when she moved another foot forward the ground seemed to shimmy just out of reach before she made contact and felt it, firm and steady again.

'Slowly, slowly catchy monkey,' she said with a smile. She was just about to take her third step when there was a blinding flash in front of her, some thirty or forty metres away. To her astonishment, a tall, deformed figure, his spacesuit specially adapted to fit his tentacled body, seemed to step out of nothingness. Janey stopped. There was no tiny rocket beside him, no visible means by which Copernicus could have arrived on his planet of gold, but he clearly had just appeared. Spotting Janey, he waved two of his tentacles impatiently and slithered away.

Janey allowed herself to breathe out. Thanks to the spacesuit, he hadn't recognized her. He must have thought she was someone else, a member of his team. As quickly as she could, Janey lunged across the sandy surface, following him.

When she reached the spot where Copernicus had appeared, she couldn't believe her eyes.

'No way,' said Janey. It couldn't be . . . but it certainly looked like . . . 'A bus stop?!' The slender pole waved in the wind, a breeze that appeared to be coming from a shimmering disc of dense air next to it. She peered more closely at the bus-stop sign, which had something printed on it in large golden letters: COPERNICUS.

Janey touched the pole gingerly, but nothing happened – although the strange wind that blew from the disc seemed to gust more strongly. Turning away, Janey stepped off in the direction Copernicus had taken. She could no longer see him, which meant that he must be inside somewhere, in a Spylab perhaps.

After several minutes, Janey found a column with

a keypad and small screen sunken into its surface. This must be the entry system to his Spylab, she thought. Yes!

There was a code to crack in order to gain entry, but Janey was not concerned. Codes and puzzles were her particular strength. She looked at the letters that blinked on the screen.

DYSYR UPIT FRDOTR

Janey looked at them again. They really didn't make any sense. She hesitated, her gloved fingers hanging over the keyboard that would allow her to enter if she could just crack the code. What should she type? Her brain clicked into action as she mentally scanned through possible solutions. And suddenly it came to her. Each of the letters in the three words was in a particular position on the keyboard. She looked to the left of D. S. To the right of Y was T. Then an S. What was to the left of that on the keyboard? 'A.' she whispered.

She continued until she had spelled out the coded message.

STATE YOUR DESIRE

Using the same code, Janey carefully keyed in the word 'ENTER': R . . . M . . . Y . . . R . . . T.

And to her joy and relief, the ground beneath

her feet gave way. She had just enough time to whip round and wave to the stream of spacesuited figures making their way from the rocket before she found herself sliding down a long tunnel.

The entry tube was obviously operated by some kind of airlock. At the bottom there was a slight pause and a loud sucking noise, before Janey – minus her spacesuit – was spat out into the Spylab.

The place was empty and Janey crept along the corridors, surprised to find that for once Copernicus's lab was not black. It was golden. Just like her new SPIsuit.

After a few minutes she came upon a vast bank of windows, very similar to the Launch Control Center she had been in just hours before. Janey peeped around the corner. There was Copernicus, pointing out various things on a screen before him to Twelve, who stared back at him with sad, dark eyes. Janey watched the boy shake his head, then drop his chin, then shake his head again, and she remembered again what G-Mamma had said about him at the beach. He couldn't speak. 'Of course!' she whispered. 'He's using sign language.'

She zoomed in with her Ultra-gogs: Twelve was repeating the same sign again. At least, it was almost the same sign. He was doing two signs rapidly, over and over: two fingers from his right hand slapped against the palm of his left, then the index finger of his right hand pointing to the fourth finger on his left. His head rattled from side to side. 'No,' she said, mimicking him. 'He's saying no.' And that must be what the signs meant. N and O. No. Two fingers on the palm – N. Fourth finger on the left hand – O.

But what was he saying no to? Janey fished out her SPI-Pod and turned up the volume. Instantly she could hear what Copernicus was saying as he pointed to the huge screen in front of him. It showed outer space, with the Earth in the distance and something like the point of an enormous pencil angled towards it.

'. . . the laser beam,' Copernicus was saying urgently. 'Just one press. We'll still be here. They'll all be there.'

N . . . O . . . signed the little boy, rattling his head back and forth.

'They won't feel anything!' Copernicus's voice was getting louder and higher. He was getting angry, Janey could tell. 'The laser beam is painless.'

But Twelve was not to be convinced, and he started to back away from his father.

A tentacle seized him around the wrist. 'Oh no you don't, boy. The first son gave up on me. I won't let you fail me too.' And he flung Twelve backwards across the floor of Mission Control.

Janey wanted to rush in and grab Twelve, but at that moment the two gorillas entered the room. Although . . . when she looked again they seemed less like gorillas and more like *men*. So he did

141

have some of his henchmen with him on the planet, and now they were picking up Twelve as if he was dropped litter and carrying him out of the room.

Janey sprinted down the corridor as fast as her Four-Fs would allow. Finally she found herself at a lift and, slapping the button, she scrambled in and closed the door just as the henchmen were rounding the corner.

She got out at the next floor and immediately heard her mother's voice. 'But it must be a dream. I've had a lot of them in the last year. Maybe it's time I saw someone . . .' It sounded as though she was in the next room, but when Janey found it empty she remembered that she still had her SPI-Pod on, amplifying the sound. It took a few minutes and the search of at least ten rooms before she found her mother, sitting on the edge of a bed talking to Leaf.

'I wonder what the whole squid thing means?' Jean Brown was saying. 'It's a recurring nightmare. Must mean something. Oh, Janey!'

Leaf spun around at the mention of her name, but Jean hardly seemed surprised that her daughter had just turned up in the middle of yet another strange hallucination.

'I have been telling your mother that this is all real,' said Leaf after he'd recovered himself, 'but she does not believe it.'

Janey ran over and gave her mum the most enormous hug imaginable. 'It is real, Mum,' she said, 'and I'm sick of lying to you and pretending, and you being the only one who doesn't know what's going on. I'm going to tell you. Leaf, mind the door, would you?'

'Sure,' he said, making sure it was closed behind him and looking out through the little glass panel.

Janey's mum frowned. 'I'm really not sure you're—'

'I am real,' interrupted Janey. 'It's all true. And I'm going to tell you. Everything.'

143

16 hand signals

Jean Brown listened without interruption as her daughter described everything that had happened since G-Mamma had first turned up at the gates of Winton School, and quite a few things that had happened before (including the fact that Jean Brown had once been Gina Bellarina, married to Superspy Boz Brilliance Brown).

'And now it looks like Copernicus has built his own planet with some Supersized bit of the core of the Earth, and he's planning on doing something terrible with a laser beam. Plus, he's been leaked the secret of R-Evolution, Dad's biggest discovery – oh, and he has all these *apes* up here too. I don't know what for,' finished Janey eventually. She looked at her mother, who hadn't moved for the best part of half an hour. 'So . . . what do you think?'

It was Leaf who first threw in a question, however. 'So Copernicus has really abandoned his own son and tried to kill him?'

'Really. Who would do that to their child?' Jean Brown's voice was barely more than a whisper.

'Mum, do you believe me?'

Jean stood up, wiping her hands down her trousers. 'Janey, what can I say? You tell me that for the best part of a year now you've been crawling in and out of the fireplace like a jack-in-a-box; that the dreadful Rosie Wotsits is your tutor or something . . .'

'SPI:KE,' said Janey and Leaf together.

'Well, whatever you want to call it,' said Jean with a toss of her head. 'And the man I'm in business with is some reincarnation of your father who isn't dead after all. It's all nonsense. It has to be. I'm caught up in one of those strange dreams again.'

'It is not a dream,' said Leaf. 'It is more like a nightmare, I suppose, but it is very real.'

Jean cast a wary eye in Leaf's direction and then turned to Janey. 'Wake me up. Wake me up now and I'll be able to forget all this.'

'But I don't want you to forget it all, Mum,' said Janey. 'I don't want to tell lies any more. And I don't want Dad to have to pretend to you either. If you know the truth, we can be a family again.'

At this Jean rolled her eyes towards the ceiling, but did a double take as they slid past the glass pane in the door. 'Oh, here we go again. Squid Man.'

With a gasp, Janey spun around. The panel was filled now by an evil yellow eye, taking in the three of them with a malevolent curiosity and more than a hint of hatred. The door slid open. 'Blonde. Again. You have a curious knack for being in the wrong place at the wrong time,' snapped the grotesque creature.

And before Janey could speak, a tentacle had coiled around her waist, and another around her mother's, and they were yanked out into the corridor. Leaf staggered after them.

'You know, for a dream monster, you actually hurt rather a lot,' barked Janey's mother, trying to struggle out of the tentacle's hold and grab Janey's hand at the same time. 'Put us down.'

At that, Copernicus simply dropped her, and Jean collapsed on the floor. 'Your wish is my command, Bellarina,' hissed Copernicus, a thin rasping sound grating from the back of his throat. 'And here's your darling Spylet daughter.'

In one smooth move he swiped his tentacle across a keypad at a nearby door, placed another tentacle on Jean Brown's back and shoved her across the glossy, polished corridor floor into the room he had just opened up. Janey was thrown in behind her and managed to forward-roll to the right so that she didn't collide with her mother. The door slammed behind them, and darkness descended.

'What is going on?' said Jean, groping for Janey's hand in the gloom. 'Are you all right?'

But before Janey could answer, her mother let out a blood-curdling scream. 'Argh! We're in a dungeon. With rats! A rat just ran across my leg. I hate rats! Hate them! Oh, it squeaked. It's coming back . . .'

Janey reflected the laser of her Girl-gauntlet on to her golden suit and a warm amber glow radiated out across the room. A small creature ventured out of the darkness. Janey reached out an arm, and the creature ran up and sat on her shoulder. 'Look, it's a monkey. A really tiny one.'

Overcoming her horror, Jean stared at it. 'I think it's a marmoset. A pygmy marmoset. We've seen them at the zoo.' She chucked it under the chin and the marmoset chattered obligingly. 'Aw. Poor little thing.'

But her words were drowned out by the sudden screeching and gibbering of a menagerie of monkeys, accompanied by some loud guttural bellows and an odd thumping sound belting out a bass line. It was like listening to a very bad school orchestra tuning up.

'Don't move,' said Janey.

'I'm going nowhere,' replied her mother with a groan. 'Except the psychiatrist's when I wake up,' she added darkly.

Handing the squirrel-sized marmoset to her mother, Janey shuffled forward. She headed for the nearest sound – a quiet gibbering that sounded more desperate than threatening – and suddenly a cage came into view. Behind the bars was a chimpanzee . . . no, several chimpanzees, their eyes wild and full of fear. 'It's OK,' said Janey softly. 'I won't hurt you.'

She did a quick headcount of the eleven chimps and moved on around the room. The next cage held a variety of smaller primates: lemurs, more marmosets, tiny tamarins with strange lion-like faces. The marmoset had obviously managed to slip between the wires of its cage.

'Janey, what are you doing? I can't see you.'

'I'm just finding out where we are and who's in here with us,' said Janey. Baboons and gibbons were in the next cage, glaring at her indignantly and then turning their backs with disdain. 'This room is massive. And it's full of apes in cages. This one's got . . . um, orang-utans, I think. And that weird thumping sound came from the gorillas.'

Jean sighed. 'So we're trapped with a bunch of wild animals. Marvellous.'

'Someone's coming!' Smothering the light from her laser by curling her finger into her palm, Janey slithered back across the room and threw herself down next to her mother.

There was a scratching sound at the door, and Janey heard her mother's breath quicken as the door handle rattled. Yet the door stayed closed. Someone was trying to get in – someone who didn't have the right codes or fingerprints to gain access. 'I bet it's the SPI team!' she whispered. 'Night vision, and zoom.'

'Pardon?' said her mother.

Janey laughed. 'Not you. My glasses. Ultra-gogs. I need to see who's at the door, and if it's Alfie or the others we can . . .'

But it wasn't one of her spy friends. It was a little boy, too small to see through the glass panel into the room from floor level. From the angle of the door handle and the peculiar sideways manner in which he was staring into the room, Janey guessed that he must be standing on the handle and hanging on to the top of the door frame. And judging by the way he moved his head from side to side, he was searching for something.

Janey felt sorry for him. He might be Copernicus's son, but so was Alfie, and it wasn't anything he was proud of. In fact, Twelve looked just as reluctant to do his father's bidding as Alfie had been. Her instincts told her that Twelve was not an enemy. She'd been wrong before, but this time Jane Blonde would have staked her life on Twelve not being on the side of evil.

'It's a little boy,' she told her mum, realizing that Jean did not have the advantage of Ultra-gogs. 'Remember the boy we saw on the beach?'

'Oh yes. The one on the rocket with us,' said Jean. She let out a brittle laugh. 'Listen to me. *The one on the rocket.* As if it was actually true!'

'He's looking for something. I'm going to help him.' Without giving herself the chance to think it through more logically, Janey pointed her laser finger at her SPIsuit and pressed. The same ambient glow filtered out across the room, and the boy's head snapped round towards her. As soon as he'd registered who she was, his face fell and he started to peer around the room again. 'Well, it's not us he's interested in,' said Janey. 'Come with me, Mum.'

Shuffling around in a close-linked pair, the marmoset still on Jean Brown's shoulder, Janey and her mother edged towards the gorilla cage. Once the two inhabitants were lit up, swaying restlessly on their enormous knuckles, Janey looked straight into the boy's eyes. He gazed at her for a moment, and then in a tiny shadow of a movement shook his head.

'Not the gorillas then.' Janey guided her mother across to the orang-utans and glanced at Twelve. Again he shook his head, glancing back along the corridor nervously before shaking his head more emphatically. 'He can hear someone coming. Quickly.' They stumbled sideways and illuminated the mesh enclosure of the smaller monkeys. No. Tears were welling up in Twelve's eyes. Janey hurried on. There was only one cage left: the chimpanzees with their quiet, desperate chattering. One was clinging to the bars at the front of the cage, and her eyes – somehow Janey knew it was a girl, another girl, like herself – glimmered in the laser light with something that could have been tears too.

And when Janey saw the expression of joy that spread up Twelve's face at the sight of the chimpanzee, she knew that they had found what he was looking for. 'It's this one,' she said, and moved closer to the cage so that Twelve would have a better view.

Jean looked for a moment, then reached out a hand to the chimpanzee's fingers. 'Poor little thing. Is it his pet, do you think?'

'Must be. He's waving.'

He was also beginning to look very panicked, Janey noticed. He waved again, turned his head to look back along the corridor and then turned to stare at Janey with such pleading in his eyes that Janey understood. These two – this boy and this chimp – wanted to be together. She knew it. When she recalled what he had drawn on the beach, she was absolutely sure. It wasn't potatoes. It wasn't food at all. It had been a clumsy attempt by a small boy to draw a chimpanzee.

But what could she do? She lifted her arms and hands, tilted her head to one side and shrugged. *It's hopeless*, she was trying to say. *I don't know what to do. Tell me how to help. Why's this one so important?*

But of course he could not speak. 'But he can use sign language,' she said suddenly. She remembered what he had signed down to the chimp in the rocket's hold earlier. Quickly she linked her pinky fingers together, tapped her fourth finger on her left hand twice, then slapped two fingers into her left palm.

Then she nodded towards the chimpanzee, as if to say, 'Shall I tell her?'

And at that moment great tears started to roll down Twelve's face. He nodded, then shrugged helplessly and whipped around to stare back down the corridor. What was it she had said? Janey knew that the two fingers and the fourth finger had spelled out NO. It was the most urgent puzzle she had ever had to work out. N was two fingers. O was a tap on the fourth finger. O was the fourth . . . something. But the fourth what?

And like a lightning strike Janey knew what it meant. O was the fourth vowel. The word he'd been spelling out ended with N, had two Os preceeding it, and the first letter was something to do with two links, formed in this case by the two little fingers joined together. 'Moon,' she said hopefully. Twelve shook his head. 'Two links . . . I . . . I don't know . . . oh! S!' she cried. 'Soon!'

Twelve nodded furiously as Jean said, 'What?'

Janey had no time to explain. 'Soon. You'll get her out soon?'

At that the boy's little face crumpled. He shook his head sadly, and Janey understood. It was too late. Janey's breath caught in her throat. The boy looked devastated. Carefully moving one hand off the door frame, he held a fist near his heart in a gesture that Janey couldn't mistake. 'You love her. I'll tell her,' she shouted, hoping he could hear her through the thick door. 'I'll tell her you love her. Is she your pet?'

But now Twelve turned around again. Someone was coming. He dropped out of sight, but just as Janey was turning to pass on his message to the chimpanzee, she saw both of his small hands in the window. He needed two hands but wasn't tall enough to see through at the same time so was reaching above his head, his back to the door so Janey could see what he was saying.

Both pinkies linked together. S.

The index finger of the right hand tapping the middle finger of the left. No idea.

Both pinkies linked again. S.

Followed by . . . a time-out sign?

Then the index finger of the right hand tapping the index finger of his left hand.

Finally, his right index finger crooked against his left palm.

Then the hands were whipped out of sight and footsteps rattled away down the corridor.

'Oh, I don't know what it means. S . . . something . . . S. SOS?' Janey spread her hands and wiggled her fingers in frustration. 'No, it can't be, because O was the fourth finger. So the fingers are vowels, and the middle finger . . . A . . . E . . . I. It's I. SIS . . .'

Janey stopped short, looking up at her mum

153

who was watching her in complete bewilderment. 'S. I. S,' she whispered. 'Then a time-out sign. Or maybe that's the sign for T. Second finger on the left hand, the second vowel. That's E. S . . . I . . . S . . . T . . . E . . .' And she put her rounded index finger in her palm as Twelve had done.

'R,' said Jean Brown, looking at the shape Janey had made. 'Definitely R. S.I.S.T.E.R. Sister. But what does he mean?'

'Sister!' Janey's voice could hardly get through her closed throat as she looked into the sad eyes of the chimpanzee. 'She's his sister.'

'But he's a boy,' said Jean.

But Janey knew the truth. 'He is now, but he wasn't always,' she said, the full horror of what she had just discovered nudging against her brain, a dark shadow, threatening, deathly. 'It's R-Evolution. Rapid Evolution. That's why Copernicus has got all these apes.'

She turned slowly to look at all the faces behind the bars. And there had been more apes on the rocket.

It was monstrous. 'He's not Twelve's father. He hasn't even given him a name. Just a number. There were twelve chimpanzees, and he was the twelfth. Copernicus *made* him, Mum. And he's got all these others here so he can put them through the R-Evolution process.'

Janey swallowed as her mother stared at her,

puzzled. 'You don't mean . . .' said Jean, slowly working it out.

'He's changing all these apes. Into humans.' Janey could hardly believe it, but she knew that Copernicus was capable of anything. 'He's making his own human race.'

And as soon as the words were out of her mouth, Janey understood what Copernicus planned to do. He would have his own breed of humans, spies, Copernicus followers. So he would have no use for the existing human race. In fact, they would simply get in the way.

Jane Blonde, for one, intended to get in the way one last time. 'Gina Bellarina,' she said urgently, 'we have to get out of here.'

With a quick smile at the startled expression in her mother's eyes, Janey headed for the gorilla cage just as someone else appeared at the door.

tube signs

As Janey released the gorillas from their cage, the door blasted open with G-Mamma, Mrs Halliday, Alfie and Tish still attached to it by their feet. The combined explosions of their Four-Fs had been enough to tear it from its hinges. Now the gorillas sprang into action, wrenching the fronts off the cages and beating out a wild, threatening tattoo on their enormous chests as they followed the other escaping primates along the corridor.

'Great gorilla bums!' From the floor, where she was still lying, G-Mamma covered her face. 'Don't let that thing stand on me!'

Janey helped her up. 'They've gone. But there are others.'

'We know that, Blonde,' said Tish. 'Two of them – well, we thought they were gorillas, but they turned out to be men – found us having a sneaky peek into Mission Control.'

'We were thrown in a huge storage room with a

load of them,' said Alfie, with a look of disgust. 'The stench was unbelievable.'

'Hmm. You've obviously never emptied your PE bag,' said his mother. 'Jean, Janey – are you both OK?'

Jean shot her a dark look, just the hint of a question hovering at the edges. 'Apart from wishing we'd gone to Bournemouth on holiday, I think we're fine.'

But Janey knew they were going to be far from fine if they didn't act quickly. 'Listen: the little boy, Twelve, is an ex-chimpanzee. Those guards used to be gorillas. Copernicus is going to R-Evolutionize all those apes into humans, and then I bet he'll try and destroy Earth with that laser beam he's got trained on it.'

'And you know all this how?' said Alfie.

Janey knew it because it all made sense. The logic, warped as it was, worked perfectly. In changing hippos into killer whales, Copernicus had been trying out the R-Evolution process. Once he'd perfected it, he'd tried it on a chimp and managed to turn it successfully – although Janey wasn't really sure if it could count as 'success' – into a little boy. He knew he could do it, and now he was shipping apes away from Earth to populate a whole new planet. It was what he'd always wanted to do. Rule the universe. He'd even made his planet golden like the sun, just to be sure everything revolved around him, the Sun King.

'There's just something I want to check,' she said as she reached for her PERSPIRE. 'Let's

157

see.' She typed '*SIGN LANGUAGE*' into the search engine and a diagram popped up showing that she'd guessed correctly. Twelve definitely had been saying 'soon', 'no', and, most disturbingly, 'sister'.

British Sign Language
Finger Spelling Alphabet

A B C D E F G H I J K L M N O P Q R S T U V W X Y Z

She showed the others.

'Far out!' Alfie whistled. 'So he *made* Twelve and now he's passing him off as his son. Hey.' A look of horror flashed across his face as a thought occurred to him. 'You don't think that I . . .'

'It would explain a lot, Monkey Boy,' said G-Mamma.

His mother snorted. 'Don't be silly, Alfie. You're perfectly normal . . . ish.'

Janey spoke quickly and decisively. 'We've got to get the other apes away from here so that they can't be R-Evolutionized too.'

'Back to Earth?' said Tish hopefully.

'I'm not sure Earth's going to last very long,' said Janey quietly. 'Get as many as you can on the rocket. There may be another way out of here . . .' When she'd seen Copernicus as she'd left the rocket, he had appeared out of nowhere. There had to be another way of coming and going from his planet. 'I'll go out and check.'

Janey ran on ahead, anxious to see what their other escape route might be, though she knew that before they escaped she'd have to find out more about Copernicus's laser beam. There was no point going back to Earth if he still had the means to destroy it. Although how a laser beam could destroy an entire planet, she wasn't sure . . .

It was only as she shot up the entry tube that

Janey realized she hadn't stopped to put on a spacesuit. Fear gripped her insides: without the protection of the suit and the gravity boots, she might well find herself launched out of the tube and straight into space. There was no way she could stop and so she thrust her SPIder between her lips and chewed furiously. If it supplied oxygen underwater, maybe it could do the same for her in space.

She popped out of the entry tube and looked around. The 'Copernicus' bus stop was just visible in the distance and she strode towards it, leaping in strange clumsy bounds as her Four-Fs ripped away from the planet and then made contact again with an odd magnetic pull. The Supersized piece of the Earth's core that stabilized this planet obviously gave it some form of gravity, but it was not quite like walking on Earth.

When she reached the bus stop she stopped and gave it a long, hard look. It wasn't a bus stop, she suddenly realized. This was more like a sign on the subway. As she looked at it, she recalled what Copernicus had said back in Florida. Back on Earth. He said he'd be taking the *tube*. Could he really have meant it? Literally? Could this possibly be a . . . tube station? The disc of air, shimmering weirdly beside her, seemed to whirl for a moment, like water disappearing down a plughole.

She couldn't risk trying it herself and there was

only one thing she was carrying that she could afford to lose. She wriggled the signal mirror out of her pocket and held it out towards the disc of moving air. The little silver circle nosed into the wind, and two things happened at once. The wind suddenly sucked so hard that Janey could barely hold on to the mirror, and in the same moment four names flashed up under 'Copernicus' on the tube sign: Moon, Canaveral, Sunny Jim's, Antarctica.

The shock of seeing the locations of Copernicus's other Spylabs made her release her grip on the mirror. The wind immediately took firm hold of the little stick and whisked it away. Janey couldn't see where exactly, but by the way the word 'Canaveral' was flashing, she guessed that the Spylab under the Kennedy Space Center was where the mirror was headed. She was so busy staring at the sign that for several moments Janey did not realize that the beeping sound in her ear was coming from one of her own SPI-buys.

'At last,' she thought, tearing off her PERSPIRE. 'An email!'

AT SPACE CENTER WITH BIRDS 'N' DIVAN. SUFFOCATING HEAT. WHERE DO WE FIND YOU? A X

Janey translated quickly. Her dad had got her SOS email, followed them to Florida with Eagle,

Peregrine, Blackbird, Rook – the Birds and Ivan Erikssen. She needed to brief him on the whole situation before the sleeping sickness caused by the heat took hold of him. Ignoring the strange grinding sensation that was juddering through the ground, Janey typed out a message.

'FIND TUBE,' she wrote. 'THERE MUST BE—'

But she never got to finish. Dropping her PERSPIRE, she ducked as a laser beam shot over her head. She looked around. There was nobody else on the surface of the planet, but just beyond the entry tube to the Spylab a giant zapper was poking out of a hole. Pointing directly at her. She had two choices. She could leap down the tube to another of Copernicus's labs, possibly ensuring her own safety. Or she could get back to the entry tube, back to the people she loved, to find another way to save the world.

It was no choice at all, really.

Stuffing her PERSPIRE back on her head, Janey crawled on her elbows as far as she could, then stood up and tried to make a run for the entry tube. She galloped across the sandy surface, launching herself as high as she could to leap over a low-flying laser beam, bounding left and right like some crazed gazelle in an attempt to dodge the radiant shots of light that were aiming directly at her. She had the entry tube in sight. She reached out to punch in the code, the code she had worked out herself, and just as she readied herself to leap away from the keypad in a perfect starjump, the laser beam caught her full in the middle and she tumbled, doubled over, into the top of the entry tube as blackness closed in around her.

laser boy

With a start, she instantly came to as the entry tube suctioned her through its lower levels and then jettisoned her neatly into the Spylab corridor. Janey checked her stomach. There was a slight warm patch – the arrow of golden light had obviously touched her, but it had not pierced her SPIsuit. In fact, she didn't feel too bad, apart from a slight need to shake her head and yawn.

The figures all around her had not fared so well, however. Piled up against the walls of the corridor, slumped wherever they had fallen, were mounds of monkeys, chimpanzees, orang-utans and gorillas.

'Oh no.' Janey spat out her SPIder and thrust it into a pocket of her golden suit as she looked around. She touched the nearest primate. It was Twelve's sister, she was sure of it. How was she going to tell him that his sister was dead? But then she felt the warmth beneath her fingers. They weren't dead. They were sedated. They had all been knocked out.

Suddenly G-Mamma careered around a corner, heading towards the entry tube like a runaway juggernaut. Janey jumped to one side, but as she did so she saw a bullet of light flash through the air, narrowly missing Alfie and Mrs Halliday, who had just followed G-Mamma into the corridor, and catching G-Mamma squarely in the back. The SPI:KE looked mildly startled for a moment, then tipped forward with her arms around the entry tube. Her eyes rolled back before closing tight, and her mauve lipstick smeared against the perspex as she slid down the tube. In less than a second, G-Mamma was sitting on the floor, wrapped around the tube as if it was some great fireman's pole, completely unconscious.

Alfie ducked then feinted left and right, pushing his mother ahead of him as they both sprinted for the entry tube. 'Watch out, JB, he's got some kind of . . . arggh!'

Janey struggled to her feet, but she was already too late. One of the glowing bullets had ricocheted off the wall and bounced right on to Alfie's chin. He clutched his face, groaned and passed out right across his mother's path. She tried to leap over his body, but in doing so she jumped into the trajectory of another blast. Now she too was slumped on the corridor floor.

Who's left? Janey thought wildly. 'Tish! Go back!' she yelled. But as she raced up the corridor she saw Tish slither out of a side corridor like a penguin sliding on ice, with her eyes shut tight and her mouth wide open in a loud snore. She'd obviously taken a full and direct hit.

What on earth – or on Planet Copernicus – could have caused such carnage?

Then she saw it: a laser beam firing from around the corner ahead of her, attached to a fat-handled gun like the super-soaker water pistols Alfie and Leaf had played with at the pool in Florida. And more shocking still, the zapper that was now firing at her was clasped firmly in a slender hand that poked from a green cuff edged with gold.

As the gun fired again, Janey dodged the laser beam and it glanced off her side.

'Leaf!' cried Janey, outraged. 'What are you doing?'

His answer was to lunge back into the corridor and shoot a couple more yellow lasers at her. She was hit in the shoulder, and then the hip, but other than a slight warmth and the need to yawn, Janey felt fine. Why were the others affected so badly when she was not?

Jane Blonde did not need to know the answer, however, to realize that she had just discovered a huge advantage. Leaf's weapon couldn't hurt her. As soon as he appeared around the corner again, Janey banged her Four-Fs against the floor and leaped at him. In less than half a second she had flown across to him, taking the full impact of a dozen *BLAM-BLAM*s from the laser gun, yet not slowing at all. Before Leaf knew what had hit him, she had ripped the gun from his hands, drop-kicked him to the floor and sat on his legs.

'You!' Janey could hardly bear to look at him. 'You're the double agent. You were the one passing the R-Evolution secrets to Copernicus.'

Staring from Janey to the laser gun she was now brandishing, Leaf gave a tiny nod.

'That's how Mum ended up here! You'd already keyed in the coordinates when I grabbed the control from you.'

'Guilty,' said Leaf, wincing as Janey squashed his knees.

'How did you get into Solfari Lands?'

Leaf swallowed, his Adam's apple bobbing up and down in his pale, slender throat. 'Satispy,' he said quietly, his eyes slightly watery as he looked up at the angry Spylet on his chest. 'I opened a hatch in the grass next to the Spylab. Nobody saw me because of the green suit.'

'And that's why you were never quite there whenever we were captured or in danger.' Janey poked him in the chest with the syringe end of the gun. 'Copernicus has been protecting you.'

Again that barely perceptible nod.

Janey felt sick. Here was yet another person she had trusted – that her father had trusted – who had turned out to be a double-crossing fake. She could not imagine what it would take to persuade someone to give up on their friends like that. 'Why, Leaf? Why would you do that? Your father has been a colleague of my dad's for decades.'

At the mention of his father, Leaf squirmed and bucked angrily, and suddenly Janey tumbled to the floor. The laser gun skidded out of her hands across the floor; she watched it skitter away, not worried about whether Leaf managed to get hold of it. It didn't seem to affect her. But when she looked around she saw that Leaf had found his feet again. He was towering over her, pale, ghost-like, with a rather large sword clasped in two hands held above his head, the tip pointing at her heart, ready to plunge right through her.

'My father was never strong enough to claim what is rightfully ours,' he spat. 'He would rather be your father's . . . employee.'

Janey stared up at the sword, trying to work out whether she had time to roll away if Leaf brought it down. There were strange symbols etched into the silver, and suddenly Janey recognized it. It was a Viking sword. Leaf was getting back to his ancestral roots.

He spoke again. 'But *I* shall not be enslaved to your father. I am a leader. Copernicus has promised me . . .'

Even as he said it, Janey saw a glimmer of doubt flit across his eyes, and she remembered him questioning how Copernicus could abandon his son. If he could do that to his own flesh and blood, what exactly were his promises worth? But Leaf shook his head as if to clear his thoughts and moved the sword even closer to Janey's ribs.

'He promised you what?' said Janey, not daring to take her eyes off the steely point that was only centimetres away from her heart.

And Leaf laughed. 'What is rightfully mine: America.'

Now Janey was convinced that Leaf, like Ariel and so many others before him – particularly Copernicus – had gone mad.

'What on earth do you mean?'

'That's exactly it, Blonde,' said Leaf, removing a hand from the sword to brush his fair hair from his eyes. The sword swung dangerously and Janey tried to suck in her stomach to avoid being skewered. 'Earth is going to be taken over by Copernicus very soon, and when that happens I will rule over America. You see,' he said gently, as if to a small child, getting a firm grip on the hilt of the Viking sword again, 'Christopher Columbus was not the first European to discover America. It was my ancestor, Leif Erikssen, who first landed on those shores. It is we Vikings who should have been the founders of the whole nation, and run the government, and ruled the world.'

There was a wild light in his eyes as he imagined the glories that should have belonged to his race.

'He tricked you, Leaf,' Janey said gently. 'Copernicus was just using you to get at my father's secrets. He's not a man of his word. You'll end up stuck on this planet. You might get to be in charge of a couple of monkeys, if you're lucky.'

Doubt flickered across Leaf's face once more, but he shook his head firmly. 'No. He has protected me. My suit . . .' and he shook his cuff so that Janey could see the golden lining slide down beneath the green outer layer, 'and the spacesuit, the place in the rocket – all this he has done to protect me.'

But Janey shook her head. 'No, Leaf. He was just protecting himself. As long as you are alive, you could pass on the secrets of R-Evolution.'

'No . . .' hissed Leaf, shaking his head to block out her words.

'It's true,' said Janey, hoping he would do something stupid as he became more emotional.

He did.

'No!' he roared, and he thrust his hands up high above his head, ready to split Jane Blonde down the middle. She had only a fraction of time, less than a second, to slither out of the way of the plunging blade, but he'd catch her, surely, if not in the heart then in a shoulder or an arm or a thigh . . . there was nowhere to go . . . no way to escape.

Knowing it was hopeless, Janey flipped on to her front, and at the very same moment she heard a familiar voice say, 'I'll take that, thank you, Leaf,' followed by a few muffled thumps and grunts and the clang of a Viking sword as it clattered to the floor.

She looked up to find Leaf bound and gagged, trussed up with a torn sheet. Someone was standing over him, the sword now pointing perilously at his throat.

'Janey,' said Jean Brown, nodding down at her daughter, 'if we're ever going to get out of here, I think I'd better start believing you. In fact, I was never sure I trusted this one,' she said. 'I was trying to tell you when you found me here, and you asked him to mind the door.'

'Mum,' said Janey in disbelief, 'you saved me! And you're all right . . . and you fought off Leaf!'

'Well, he's just a boy really, and I am a super-SPI, darling,' said Jean Brown, looking down at her neat T-shirt and trousers as if she still couldn't believe it. 'Apparently,' she added.

It was harder still for Janey to believe. She'd hoped beyond all hope that her mum could believe what she'd told her, but somehow she'd never been terribly convinced that her mother would accept the truth. 'What changed your mind?'

'Ah, well, yes,' said Jean. 'I got left behind down the corridor so I was wandering around, trying to find you, and I went past this room with big windows. Squid Man was inside, and there was a great big screen with a huge one of these just showing on it.' She nudged the laser gun with her toe. 'Anyway, as I was watching, the picture sort of zoomed in and I realized we were looking at Florida, at that Space Center place. And then it zoomed in even closer and there on the floor was . . . your father.'

Janey gasped. Her mum knew!

'And the funny thing was, when I saw him there on the floor, knocked out, surrounded by all these other people dressed in peculiar spy-type gear, my insides went all funny and I shouted out . . . well, I shouted, "Boz!". Rather loudly.'

Janey had never felt happier. Her mum believed her! She knew everything! 'Oh, Mum,' she said with a sob, 'we can be a family again.'

Jean dropped the sword and crouched down. 'Not if we don't stop old Squid Man,' she whispered. 'He's up to something terrible, I know it.'

Janey knew it too. The end of the Earth. The beginning of a new regime. Copernicus ruling from Planet Copernicus.

'Mum, wake the others up. There's a weird disc of wind near a "Copernicus" tube stop just outside the entrance – I know it sounds crazy, but jump in it, all of you, and get off at the moon. There's another Spylab there.'

Her mother looked at her, opened her mouth to say something, then shrugged. 'Landing on the moon is really no more outrageous than anything else I've been through in the last few days. I'll make sure we've all got our spacesuits on. But what will you do, Janey? I mean . . . Blonde?'

Janey didn't know whether to laugh or cry, but there was no time for either.

'I'm going to save the Earth,' she said. And throwing her super-SPI mum a kiss, she sprinted away down the corridor, to the centre of all problems.

Mission Control.

Copernicus.

laser beam

The foul and disfigured Copernicus stood at the heart of Mission Control. Janey groaned as she saw who was standing next to him: Twelve.

She turned on her SPI-Pod. 'I don't have the manpower to round up all those escaped gibbering animals,' lisped Copernicus to the little boy, 'but I still have my SPI-clone machine. If they all escape, I'll make clone copies of you, Twelve. I'd better warn you though,' he added as if he actually cared for the boy, 'that the master version doesn't fare very well. You'll get all used up. Very quickly.' The great shoulders of the hideous creature jiggled up and down. He was laughing.

Janey looked directly at the screen – and her stomach heaved. There was her father, lying unconscious on a floor somewhere. The image on the screen zoomed out and Janey could now see that her dad was lying next to the Bird SPI family and Leaf's father, Ivan Erikssen. When the image zoomed out even further Janey could see the whole of Cape Canaveral. Then the Florida coastline and the entire east coast of America. And all the time the rocket-length tip of the giant laser beam pointed accusingly down at the Earth. She instructed her Ultra-gogs to zoom in on the laser and she noticed for the first time that there was writing along the side of it. Next to an embossed sun were the words LAY-Z BEAM.

Laser beam. She knew that already. Why was he directing it at the Earth? Would it actually kill?

Jane Blonde looked left and right. There was nobody around to stop her, but no obvious way into Mission Control either. Then it came to her. There was a very obvious way to enter Mission Control. After turning her SPI-Pod to 'MIC' for microphone, she lifted her bare left hand and hammered on the glass.

Copernicus spun around, a grotesque maypole of whirling limbs and flapping black cloth, his severed jaw hanging looser still at the sight of his nemesis. 'B-Blonde!' He could barely stand to utter her name, so outraged was he at the sight of her standing there, leaning on the window frame and shouting out to the boy: 'Twelve, get away from him! Run!'

It went just as she had planned. Infuriated, Copernicus stumbled towards the glass and lashed out with one of his enormous, grime-encrusted tentacles. Amplified by Janey's SPI-Pod microphone, the sound of the glass shattering made Janey drop to her knees, grasping at her ears. In that moment Copernicus struck, and the next thing she knew, Janey had been gripped around the middle by a pulsating tentacle and was whistling through the air, straight down into Mission Control.

She slammed on to the floor with a bone-crunching smack. 'Watch them, then!' Copernicus was screaming hysterically. 'Watch them all lose the will to live! Everyone you've ever known, Blonde! Everyone you've ever loved! They're all down there, all sucking up to your ridiculous father and his do-gooding types, when they should be listening to me! Me! Well, now they will. Now they will have no choice. No voice of their own. Now they will have . . . NO WILL!'

His hideous limbs thrashed like some insane conductor as he pointed at the screen and flung Janey from his grasp. His shrieking filled her entire head so that it felt like it would explode. Eyes scrunched up against the pain, Janey ripped off her SPI-Pod and threw it to one side. Relief came instantly. She could now hear that Twelve was sobbing gently, shuffling back as far as he could under a bench, while a python-like tentacle reached out for her. It grabbed her by the ankle, and Janey suddenly found herself hanging upside down, facing the screen.

'Rotate one-eighty degrees!' she yelled at her Ultra-gogs, and at once she could see the screen properly. The image had shifted once more. No longer was it showing the coast of America; now the whole of that continent lay before her, and then there was the whole Earth, tilted below them like the globe in her classroom. Her lovely, ordinary classroom, in lovely, ordinary Winton School. Red figures were illuminated in the right-hand corner. 60. 59. 58.

The one-minute countdown was on.

'Twelve!' she screamed. 'Jump! Get up to the window; get out and go to the tube station. Find the others. Go! Go!'

With a frantic and fearful glance at Janey's upside-down face, Twelve took his chance and leaped on to the workbench. He then flung himself, monkey-like, up to a dangling light shade and swung across to the shattered window. After a last glance in her direction, he was gone.

Pulling herself up as far as she could, Janey sank her teeth into the hideous tentacle that was holding her captive, and Copernicus threw her to one side and drew in his tentacle limb in the same movement.

'Nasty girl. Anyway. Thirty seconds,' he gloated. 'Ah, look.'

Staring over at the screen, Janey saw that the Lay-Z Beam was pointed at the North Pole. The top of the world. She said the words 'Lay-Z Beam' out loud. And immediately she understood what Copernicus was doing.

It wasn't a laser beam as such. It was a *lazy*

177

beam. He'd been directing it at Florida for weeks. That was why everyone was falling asleep. Losing the will to do anything. That's what had been affecting her team. And now he was going to cover the Earth with apathy and laziness and the complete loss of will to do anything to resist him.

A Lay-Z Beam. It was almost brilliant, thought Janey. Copernicus didn't actually have to kill anyone. They'd just all be too sleepy and forgetful to bother to live any more.

Twenty seconds showed on the screen, the tip of the Lay-Z Beam starting to glow bright amber. The colour reminded Janey of something. Her suit.

And in the very instant that she recalled how the Lay-Z Beam had never affected her, she climbed on the workbench, slammed her feet on to it, powered out through the window and Four-F'd towards the entry tube.

Copernicus threw back his monstrosity of a head and laughed.

But Janey knew she had a tiny chance. With fifteen seconds to go, she could just save the world.

20 a ray of light

It had to work.

As she shot up the entry tube, Janey pulled off one of her Four-Fs and roughly shoved her SPIder into her mouth. The front legs snaked out between her lips, clamping around her nose, as the other six legs anchored themselves over her gums and pumped oxygen down her throat. Her head hit the surface and she was flung out on to the sandy surface of Planet Copernicus. There could only be a few seconds left. The whole of the planet vibrated beneath her feet. Janey looked around frantically and spotted the great, glowing amber orb, attached to the end of the Lay-Z Beam like the venom at the tip of a bee sting. She skidded towards it and could just make out a shining blue-and-white globe coming into view below her.

The golden orb was pulsating. It was gathering strength. Janey suddenly had the impression of a giant drawing its breath, ready to snuff out an enormous candle. Only this time, she thought, the candle was the Earth.

Planet Copernicus shuddered beneath her as it prepared to launch its attack of sleeping sickness upon the world.

Hardly realizing what she was doing but knowing that it was the world's only chance, Jane Blonde bent down, ripped off her remaining Four-F spy shoe and thrust herself up and out, straight into the atmosphere, floating free in just a golden SPIsuit and a peaked PERSPIRE hat.

In outer space.

I'm completely mad, she thought.

The end of the Lay-Z Beam was right below her. With a powerful breaststroke action Janey pulled herself through space – now she *knew* she was mad. She was actually swimming through space. The golden beam, quivering with scorpion evil, was next to her . . . above her . . . pointing right at her.

She could see the Earth. Janey couldn't help drawing in a breath at the beauty of the world below her, a tiny bead of decoration on the soft quilt of the universe.

But then a sensation of immense pressure made her turn over, away from the planet she was trying to save, looking back at the planet she had just launched herself from. The golden orb of light appeared before her, bright as the sun, and then suddenly it was streaming towards her. Closing her eyes, she wriggled slightly to the right and waited for the impact.

The full power of the Lay-Z Beam hit her directly in the stomach, enveloping her in a burning cloud of acid-yellow light. The pain was immense. It was like being swallowed alive by the sun . . . heat – unbearable heat – and blinding, agonizing light that seemed to cut through to the back of her brain, severing it in two, splitting her head apart . . .

And suddenly Janey realized the sensation of movement was not just limited to her stomach or her head. She was hurtling, free-falling through space, eyes closed against the awful brilliance of the Lay-Z Beam that had seemed somehow to become part of her. The SPIder was slipping from her mouth . . . she couldn't breathe . . . couldn't see . . . couldn't survive . . .

She was dying. Janey knew it. This was it, for once and for all. Spinning, flipping, sailing through the atmosphere, she reached out a hand towards the beautiful blue planet beneath her. Earth. She could see it. One last time . . .

Then there was a flash and a crushing sense of pressure. At that moment her feet whipped round over her head; she looked back through her knees and there was Planet Copernicus, brighter and more golden than ever, shimmering in the haze of the treacherous Lay-Z Beam blast reflected directly off her golden SPIsuit, straight back at the source of its evil. As she shielded her eyes from the glare there was a gathering of light, an explosion that zapped out a cloudburst of phosphorescence, and a crescent of brilliance crowned Planet Copernicus like an eclipse. At once the golden planet faded to grey.

The reign of Copernicus was over.

A second later there was another flash, nearer this time. And something tiny and white came into view. Something she couldn't quite believe she could be seeing. And then Jane Blonde's brain and the golden light blurred into one, and she knew nothing more.

21 goldenspy

Janey woke up in a hospital bed, still convinced that she was dead, with a whole team of SPIs and Spylets around her and Trouble curled up at her feet. Perhaps they were all dead too. They must be. She'd fainted.

But seeing Janey's eyes open, her SPI:KE threw herself on to the bed and crushed Janey to her bosom. 'She's ALIVE! She'll SURVIVE! Oh, sizzling sunsets, I can't help myself – I'm rapping even when I don't know I'm doing it. But I'm just so HAPPEEEEEEE.' She plastered Janey's cheeks with sticky magenta kisses until someone had the presence of mind to pull her off.

'You're not dead then?' said Alfie in his flat voice. Janey could see by the way he was twisting his lips that he was trying not to smile.

'I'm not sure,' said Janey. She checked her limbs under the sheets. Apart from being in some very scratchy singed spandex, they seemed fine. 'Are you?'

'Du-uh.' Alfie held out his arms and spun around. 'Definitely not.'

'We're all alive and well, thanks to you, Blonde,' said Mrs Halliday, patting Janey on the hand.

Memories came back to her in a flood: her mum, finally believing her; her dad, Lay-Z Beamed on the ground at Cape Canaveral; the apes, the spies, Twelve, heading off for the tube. 'Dad . . . Mum . . .' she croaked suddenly.

'We're here, sweetheart,' said her mother.

We? Did she really mean . . . *we?*

The others cleared a path so that Janey's parents could reach her bedside. To her astonishment, her father had his arm around her mum's shoulders, and Jean Brown had a definite air of something . . . something *spyish* about her.

Jean pulled Janey up from the bed and squeezed her shoulders. 'I thought you were right behind. That tube just sucked me off Planet Copernicus and deposited me at the moon station in seconds. I thought you'd be following.'

'I had things to do,' said Janey. She looked at her father. 'Did you know about the tubes?'

He sighed. 'There's been talk for many years of tubes in space that we could travel through. Wormholes . . . gravitational corridors . . . Whatever you want to call them, they form a network of invisible tunnels. What I can't believe is that Copernicus learned to harness their power before anyone else did.' He leaned over and kissed her cheek, adding quietly, 'These NASA scientists are very keen to talk to you about it.'

'NASA? We're still at Cape Canaveral, then?'

Tish leaned over Abe's shoulder. 'Blonde, you discovered an unknown planet. Oh, and destroyed it. Of course we're still at Cape Canaveral.'

'That's what woke us all up,' said her father with a grin. 'That, and Ronnie dropping Trouble on my stomach with his sabre claw out.'

Janey still didn't understand.

'I . . .'

It didn't seem possible, somehow, but she remembered now the golden beam ricocheting off her golden suit, the flash of light behind her . . . 'Did I blow it up? Is Copernicus dead?' And Leaf, she thought. It saddened her. Leaf had been duped by Copernicus, but he'd looked as though he might just be reaching the point of changing his mind about his allegiances . . .

'Titian's exaggerating,' said her mother. 'You didn't destroy it. You just put it to sleep. Come see.'

Like a travelling circus troupe, a dozen SPIs and Spylets accompanied Janey as she levered herself off the bed and made her way gingerly along the corridor. They passed a couple of burly security guards – who looked nothing like gorillas, Janey was glad to see

– and found themselves at the end of a corridor. Two doors faced each other, both with another security guard outside with NASA emblazoned on their uniform.

At a nod from her father, Janey opened the door to her right. On a starkly made-up bed lay a crumpled body, snoring rudely. Leaf's SPIsuit lay on a chair nearby, and Janey picked up the tattered Lycra with its layers of green and gold. 'That's what made me realize I should jump in front of the Lay-Z Beam,' she said slowly. 'I hadn't been affected by the rays like everyone else, and Leaf said he was OK too because of his suit. It had to be the gold. There was that man at Disney World in the yellow shirt, and the lady in the yellow sundress – they seemed protected too.'

'That's right. Copernicus must have worked it out when you weren't being affected, and then Leaf went into overdrive to get you to do anything where you might get changed.'

'Volleyball! Swimming!' It made sense now.

Abe nodded. 'The scientists think that because he was wearing it when the beam blasted back at the planet, he might not sleep forever. He could wake up in a while.'

It was only then that Janey noticed the figure to the other side of Leaf's bed. Ivan stood up with his head bowed and reached out to shake Janey's hand. 'I can only apologize for my son's behaviour, as I have done to your father a million times.'

'Two million and counting,' shouted G-Mamma from the back of the crowd.

'I will stay here with Leaf until he wakes up, and then we will consider our future.' Ivan shrugged pitifully. 'At least it is a future on this planet. Thanks to you, Blonde.' He raked his hands through his thinning hair and sat down again.

'There's something else to see,' said her father gently, and they all shuffled out of the room, making way so that Janey could get to the door of the ward opposite. 'This person was dressed in black, so he didn't have the golden-spy protection. It's believed that he will sleep for a long time. Perhaps forever – if we're lucky.'

Janey pushed open the door. There was no bed in this room. Instead there was a specially created tank, and sealed upright inside was the drooped and sleeping figure of a strange half-squid, half-human figure, with one eye huge and yellow, and the other human eye closed tight shut. Jets of water were spurting over him, keeping his foul skin moist. Despite being sound asleep, the expression of the bleak squid eye still managed to look shocked, outraged.

'That eye's golden,' said Janey quietly. 'It might wake up.'

'It's blind,' said her father. 'And we'll never let him out of our sight again.'

Janey closed the door. Suddenly she felt exhausted. 'How long was I asleep?'

187

'About a week,' said Mrs Halliday as they walked back towards Janey's room. 'You might have had the golden SPIsuit, but you still took the entire blast from the Lay-Z Beam yourself.'

'But how did I . . . I was just floating around in space, and then I saw this flash and a little white . . . a little white . . .'

At exactly that moment she spotted again what she had seen in space. A small white hand. Waving to her. Beckoning. This time it was waving from the doorway of her own ward.

Jean Brown hugged her. 'It was Twelve, although we've decided to call him James. We can't go on calling him by a number forever.'

'Forever?'

'It's too dangerous to try to D-Evolve him,' said her father softly. 'And I never want to use R-Evolution again, so we can't change his sister for him. We're all the family he's got – and he did save you, after all.'

'We're . . . adopting him?' Janey looked from her parents to the little boy with the dark solemn eyes, gazing at her from the bedroom door. 'How did he save me?' she whispered.

'Well, it was hard to work out what he wanted,' said her mother. 'None of us know sign language. But he got me to grab his ankle, then he dangled out into space and grabbed you as you went by. Brave boy.'

'True spy material,' agreed her father.

As the other spies fell silent, Janey walked over to James. He raised his eyebrows, and Janey just knew, instinctively, what he was asking.

She nodded, a tear spilling over on to her cheek. 'Yes, I'm OK. Thanks to you.'

He gave a small smile, and then started tapping out sign language.

'Oh, you're too fast for me. I'll have to learn . . . hang on. You're telling me you're called James.'

With a huge grin he nodded enthusiastically. Janey crouched down in front of him. 'Do you know who I am?'

His rapid sign language contained at least an A, an N and an E. 'Janey. Yes, but not just that.'

And on her knees in front of him, she pointed at herself and then at the boy and lifted up her hands.

Both pinkies linked together.

The index finger of the right hand tapping the middle finger of the left.

Both pinkies linked again.

A time-out sign.

The index finger of the right hand tapping the index finger of her left hand. Finally, her right index finger crooked against her left palm.

'Sister,' she whispered.

James's eyes became bright with tears and he flung himself into Janey's arms. When she turned around to look at the others, Janey noticed that she and

James weren't the only ones looking a little teary. Even Alfie was clearing his throat and trying to look very interested in a placard about the misuse of mobile phones in technical areas.

Janey grinned. She was the luckiest girl in the world. And as if on cue, G-Mamma held up her hands and rotated slowly to gather attention.

'A little rap to celebrate,' she said. 'Alfie and Rook, do this: Dum dum chich. Dum dum chich.'

'Yeah, right,' said Alfie.

'Baby Halo . . .' warned G-Mamma.

With a scornful roll of his eyes, Alfie said in a monotone, 'Dum dum chich. Dum dum chich.'

'Great! Now Blackbird and Titian, you can go BADA in between the dum dum chiches.'

Tish and Blackbird looked at each other, shrugged and joined in with enthusiasm. With the dum dum chich BADA, dum dum chich BADA rhythm going on behind her, G-Mamma swayed hypnotically.

> 'The goldenspy, she did survive,
> She stayed alive, now gimme high five;
> The goldenspy is Blonde all through,
> It's what she do, lemme hear ya OO OO;
> Goldenspy! Taking out the yellow eye.
> Goldenspy! Through the heavens she can fly.
> Goldenspy! Brown and Blonde rolled up in one.
> Goldenspy! And she only just begun . . .'

G-Mamma and her little backing group hopped away down the corridor, and Janey watched them leave. She stretched happily and yawned. This had been the most exhausting holiday ever. Which reminded her of something . . . 'Am I ready to leave hospital yet, Mum?'

Her mother tilted her head suspiciously. 'It's much too soon for another mission, Jane Blonde.'

And Janey smiled back at her mum, taking in her parents and her new little brother in a golden glow all of her own. This was going to be a completely different kind of mission. A new adventure.

'Let's go home,' she said.

Find out how it all began . . .

Jane Blonde

'Until now, you have been just plain old Janey Brown. But you are going to grow and grow. You will be what your parents have not allowed you to be. It's in your past. And it's in your future. There's a whole new part of you just waiting to you to burst out. You are Jane Blonde – Sensational Spylet. Welcome to our world.'

Follow Jane Blonde on her first non-stop mission!

Jane Blonde
spies trouble

Jane's purr-ecious spy-cat, Trouble, has been kidnapped! A group of mad scientists think they have discovered the secret to a cat's nine lives – but they need Trouble for their experiments. All the clues lead down the drain – spying can be a wet and stinky business! But with chewing gum that lets her breathe underwater, a SPIpod tracking device and a high-speed mini-hover-board, Jane Blonde is ready for ACTION . . .

Jane Blonde
twice the spylet

Jane Blonde, Sensational Spylet, has just met her secret twin!

When the sisters are posted to an Australian sheep farm, Janey's instincts are on red alert. There's something weird about those sheep. Come to think of it, there's something suspicious about Jane Blonde's twin . . .

Janey can raise an invisible shield with her spy-ring and she can burrow through the earth with her spy-drill boots – but will incredible gadgets save her this time?

Jane Blonde
spylet on ice

Jane Blonde, Sensational Spylet, is hurled on her coolest mission yet when she enrols at SPIcamp!

There are gadgets galore at the top-secret facility and there's even a snowdome where the spylets can chill out. And when the team is sent on a mysterious polar expedition, Janey's spylet-training – and her new snowboard skills! – are put to the test.

A selected list of titles available from Macmillan Children's Books

The prices shown below are correct at the time of going to press. However, Macmillan Publishers reserves the right to show new retail prices on covers, which may differ from those previously advertised.

JILL MARSHALL

Jane Blonde	978-0-330-43814-8	£5.99
Jane Blonde Spies Trouble	978-0-330-43825-4	£5.99
Jane Blonde, Twice the Spylet	978-0-330-44657-0	£5.99
Jane Blonde, Spylet on Ice	978-0-330-44658-7	£5.99

All Pan Macmillan titles can be ordered from our website, www.panmacmillan.com, or from your local bookshop and are also available by post from:

Bookpost, PO Box 29, Douglas, Isle of Man IM99 1BQ

Credit cards accepted. For details:
Telephone: 01624 677237
Fax: 01624 670923
Email: bookshop@enterprise.net
www.bookpost.co.uk

Free postage and packing in the United Kingdom